GIANT TALES

WORLD of
PIRATES

Professor Limn Books

Giant Tales
Beyond the Mystic Doors

Giant Tales
From the Misty Swamp

Giant Tales
World of Pirates

CRYSTAL SWORD CHRONICLES:
GRYFFON MASTER

GIANT TALES
3-MINUTE STORIES

WORLD of
PIRATES

Introduction by
PROFESSOR K.R. LIMN

Professor Limn Books
Charlotte, North Carolina

For information, please write to: H. M. Schuldt
www.writers750.com

Cover Art © 2013 by Northlake Art Studio
Interior Art Design © 2013 Northlake Art Studio
Each author holds the copyright to their own story.

First published in 2014 by Professor Limn Books
ISBN 978-0-9885784-5-6

PERMISSION
Each author from WORLD OF PIRATES
owns their individual story and
has given official written permission
to place their story/stories in this anthology for publication.

First Edition, January 2014

For those with the spirit of
Alvilda,

a traveler who left behind
cozy royal robes of fox and squirrel
to find those who seek adventure

Preface

This anthology is a work of fiction
written by forty authors.
Each story in chapter one
is based on a pirate theme
where each tale includes
a bad boy pirate, rum, and money.
A suggested story prompt was given in an
online fiction group, writers750.com,
with the purpose of creating
a new and original short story.
Giant Tales: World of Pirates
has a second chapter,
A Light In the House,
where the theme is perseverance.
Each story in this chapter
is based on a story prompt,
which includes a house, a light,
and a musical sound from another realm.
Authors from this book are welcome
to add on to their own short story
and turn their own tale into a novel.
These tales are brilliantly crafted,
an imaginative and unusual blend of
admiration and sticking with it.

PROFESSOR K.R. LIMN

Contents

CHAPTER ONE
PIRATES

CHAPTER TWO
A ℒIGHT IN THE HOUSE

AFTERWORD

1. Jenise Erikson
2. Randy Dutton
3. Mike Boggia
4. Peter Coster
5. Mary Agrusa
6. Colleen Sayre
7. Christian Warren Freed
8. Scott Amis
9. Arlene Lagos
10. Harry Alexiou
11. Joyce Shaughnessy
12. Gail Harkins
13. Randall Lemon
14. H.M. Schuldt
15. Lynette White
16. Sylvia Stein
17. Janet Bond
18. Alli Vaughan
19. Mirta Oliva
20. Elaine Faber

*A*FTERWORD

INTRODUCTION

Drink up, my hearties, to all my ardent shipmates! If you'd like to hear a pirate tale, then this is the book for you. By all that is great and good, forty authors in this book have been to the place of Davy Jones' locker and lived to tell the tale. So now, Giant Tales reader, good fortunes await as you dive into fifty-three tales of bad boy pirates and surprising resolutions. An ancient curse is causing ships to sink in the Caribbean, and treasure is to be found. You will be pleasantly engaged to find roving adventure with desperadoes and voyagers sailing near uncharted islands. Life is merry for outlaws who live but a short life as pirates in the brotherhood of the coast.

Giant Tales: World of Pirates brings you chapter one, *Pirates*, which includes thirty-seven seafaring tales of wandering survivors and scavengers o' the deep. Chapter two, *A Light In the House*, offers you sixteen more delightful tales of mysterious characters who live in strange places where it might be easy to give up. In this collection of short stories, you will find themes of admiration and perseverance, so let us drain a goblet and take in a new world. I wish you a fair wind ever and always as you heave up your anchor and enjoy reading this marvelous book. Good fortune with you and yours!

PROFESSOR K.R. LIMN

CHAPTER ONE

PIRATES

THE SEA QUEEN

by
Jenise Erikson

Of all the galleons in all the ports in the entire world, he walks onto mine. A beard as black as the aphotic depths, braided and adorned with red ribbon, he was tall with a powerful physique, an earring in his left ear. Blimey. When he spoke, I knew we'd be drinking grog together before the night was over. My gaze was interrupted. "A doubloon for yer thoughts?"

"You must be my new quartermaster," I said, reaching for his hand. "Welcome to the Sea Queen, Mr...."

The gruff voice spoke. "Aye, Captain. Me name's Morgan. Stede Morgan. I came to the Sea Queen to see the desert."

"The desert? What desert? We're headed into open waters."

"I was misinformed."

I led Mr. Morgan to his quarters. "Grub is served at six o'clock," I said, and headed to my cabin. I threw my hat on the beddi, pulled off my heavy overcoat, and shrugged out of my Coxon shirt. The cloth around my breasts had begun to slide. I lifted the girls and tightened the strap. I selected a loose shirt and concealed it with a vest. Retrieving my captain's hat, pulling it low, I opened the door. A forceful wind greeted me. It unsaddled my hat then spate down the gangway. Straightening my disguise, I flung the mess hall door open.

All hands were lounging in the forecastle. I spotted Stede sitting alone, downing a pint. I filled a mug with rum and water and sat down next to the new quartermaster. He said, "I 'ear ye scored quite the booty in Barbados last week, aye?"

"That we did. How'd you hear of it?"

"The Desert told me," he said smiling. A flush warmed my face as his eyes bore through me. I glanced down, fidgeting with my vest buttons. Suddenly a grip compressed around my wrist, and Stede jerked me to him. I felt cold steel in my ribs. The confined room quieted when four deckhands drew their cutlasses. Stede muttered softly, "Now where's the loot, matey?" The four traitors forced the other sailors on the floor and bound their hands with a cato'nine tails. Stede shoved me from the room, commanding as we left, "Desert Fists Collier! Throw the crew in the bilge."

"Aye, aye, Captain!" Desert said.

Stede's dagger guided me to my quarters, and he closed the door behind us. I asked, "Who are you really?"

"Aye, no questions. There's no time for it. Pull up the planking under yer bedding and hand me the gold."

Suddenly the hull rolled starboard, and Stede lost his footing. I broke away and staggered toward the door, escaping into the gangway. The ship rolled to the port and pinned me to the wall. I fought my way up the ship's ladder and out to the lifeboat, loosening the rigging.

A muffled demand reached me through the windstorm as the boat hit the water. "Stay put, me beauty!"

I glanced around, backing away towards the railing. I hollered, "How'd you know!" Stede charged me, seized my waist, and swept me over the ship's side, falling into the tumultuous waters.

I awoke shivering in the arms of the bilge rat who'd tainted my crew. My wet hair clung to my cheeks as I lifted my head from his hairy chest. "Land ahoy," he whispered. I scanned the horizon and sighted a small island.

"How'd you know?"

"Let's see, the last time we met…"

I stared at his rugged face searching for answers. "…was Kingston." Queen Anne's war. My father had hired the young privateer to prey on the French for the British army. Lean, clean-shaven, and young, I hardly recognized the older version.

"We'll always have Kingston," he said, his brown eyes enveloping me with warmth.

"How'd you find me?" I said.

"The whole world was crumbling around us back then. We'd picked a bad time to fall in love. I decided to do the thinking fer both of us. When me first mate discovered yer whereabouts, he joined yer crew. He discovered ye 'ad a bounty on yer head and yer crew were gonna turn on ye. I knew it were time fer me to make me move."

"They'll find me," I said.

"The island tis drawing us closer. The curse of St. Anne tis upon me. Ere, take ye treasure," he said, handing me the Spanish dubloons. "Me Desert will meet ye at the shore. Here's lookin' at you, lassie." And he disappeared over the edge of the lifeboat.

An Afterword to this story is on page 227.

SMITHY'S ORGAN

by
Randy Dutton

Jerome spat out black sand and rolled onto his back. He looked at the fading stars while warm salty waves lapped over his reef-scratched thighs. How long had he clung to wreckage in this Caribbean lagoon? He sat up. Sunrise was coming. Only one of the barque's three masts was visible above the reef. He listened for the ethereal music they had heard hours earlier, the siren's song that had lured his captain closer to shore. There was nothing but the crash of waves slowly grinding the ship's carcass apart. Nearby, flotsam cluttered the lagoon. The onshore wind had blown the cargo inland, but there were no bodies… anywhere.

"Ahoy!" yelled a man in a white silk blouse and black trousers from atop a volcanic outcrop. A cutlass hung from his belt and a coil of rope looped around his neck and arm. Jumping onto the sand, he ran past the half-drowned Jerome, cheering, "Begad, me fortune be good this day!" He stopped and turned – the young man was staring at him. "Avast me matey! Di' ye have any wenches aboard?"

Jerome shook his head.

"'Tis a shame, it now being just us two."

"No other survivors?" Jerome asked sadly, considering the loss of his shipmates.

The man shook his head. "Ye be t' cabin boy?"

Jerome nodded.

"I be Smithy. Give a hand, me bucko before t' tide takes me booty past t' reef." He took off running.

Jerome slowly stood. The stranger splashed into the waves and swam past the first few crates bobbing near the rocky shore. "Ayeeaaaa!" Smithy cried out, as he pulled his rope lashed to a rum cask. "I be rich!

Jerome helped the strange man haul what drifting cargo they could onto shore, and then to an elaborate shelter hidden inland. Its furnishings and ornamentation were derived from several shipwrecks.

Nightfall came with a rising full moon as they feasted on salted pork around a blazing fire.

"Splice the mainbrace!" Smithy downed his second mug while flipping a doubloon.

Jerome tipped back his own, then exclaimed, "From the ship, we heard music, but now it's gone…"

"Aye, me siren's organ be still this night."

"Your o-r-g-a-n?"

Smithy tossed a bit of ash into the air to watch its drift, then smiled. He stood and tilted his head toward the volcanic rocks. They walked up a worn path onto a black lava shelf that reached into the water. Jerome's brow furrowed at the sight of seven parallel long timbers each lying across a fulcrum. At the end of each lever, a cannon ball was attached. "This be me organ!" Smithy said proudly as his nose lifted into the onshore breeze. "Heave on thar timber."

Jerome pulled on the first lever's free end, lifting the cannon ball off a carved borehole and was greeted with a high-pitched musical note as a blast of air rushed out. He dropped the ball back in its socket. He heaved on each timber and was rewarded with different notes. "Amazin'! Did ya do this?"

"Aye, lad. I chiseled through t' rock to sea caves below."

"So the wind feeds your organ?"

"Ye be a bright lad. Aye, if t' wind be right. And when a ship be near, I plays me chantey."

"But when a ship hits the reef, people die!"

Smithy shrugged. "People die all t' time."

Jerome sadly shook his head. "Too bad ye didn't git the brigantine that whar chasin' us."

Smithy's brow lifted. "Ye whar chased?" His eyes widened. "By treasure seekers?"

"Uh huh. They tried boardin' but we hoisted too much sail."

"So they think they still be astern ye." He rubbed his chin and grinned. "And this be their quickest route." He pulled out a spyglass. "Sail ho! Lad, let me teach ye a ditty."

The moon had reached its zenith when the brigantine's quarterdeck became visible. Jerome pulled down each timber in the pattern he had been taught, the sounds nearly deafening him.

"Shiver me timbers!" Smithy exclaimed as the ship abruptly stopped, then heeled hard to port. "Belay t' pipes!" The sound of cracking wood and swearing sailors indicated more prey had been caught in his snare. Smithy twirled a cutlass in his right and jabbed another in the sand next to the rope. "Smartly thar, matey. Give them scalawags no quarter, or ye haul in t' swag. Choose."

Jerome's eyes widen. He grabbed the rope.

Smithy smiled. "And lad... save any wenches!"

An Afterword to this story is on page 228.

3

THE CARIBBEAN GODDESS

by
Mike Boggia

Aycayía's song bewitched us, and our ship ran aground on the volcanic reef at the edge of the Bermuda Triangle. The greedy waves ripped her apart in less than five minutes, and we swam for our lives. I threw my arm around a barrel of rum and let the wind and waves carry me where they would, resigned to die on sharp rocks or drown. Better this, than hung as a picaroon.

I clung to the cask until I passed out. I awoke on a small patch of white sand, my rum butt beside me. I got to my knees and scouted the island. It had traces of volcanic lava dotted with patches of tropical vegetation.

A tattered emaciated brigand I didn't recognize staggered out of the trees and came toward me. He held a homemade fishing spear in his hand.

"Trade yer fer rum, Matey." His eyes rolled in his head. He dropped the spear and fell to his knees. "Fer the love of yer mudder, rum, man." He took the tin cup clipped to his belt and held it in trembling hands.

I filled it. He downed the rum in a gulp and extended the mug.

"Glad ye came, ye scurvy excuse for a buccaneer. Look yonder, by the lone tree. All the gold ye'd ever crave, in that thar chest. It's yer's, boyo. Thankee for givin me freedom courage to 'scape."

He got to his feet, dropped the cup, and ran into the breakers. I watched him bob out of view. The old marauder was loony.

I heard Aycayía's song, haunting and luring me into the jungle. I found her waiting for me in front of a thatched hut, the most beautiful lass ever to grace the earth. She didn't have to smile and beckon twice to get me to do whatever she asked.

In the evening, I speared fish with the gift the buccaneer left. She cooked them, and we dined and drank rum. She wanted to remain with me forever, and I was willing. Shipwrecked with a goddess, what more could I wish for?

For a few weeks, I wondered why the crazy galley rat ran into the sea, when food, rum, gold, and gorgeous Aycayía were satisfying my life. Ah, paradise for this freebooter, mates.

But one night she left our hut, and I followed her. I watched her climb a peak where she sang her most alluring song. The next morning I found that she had called a sailor onto the beach.

"Glad to see ya, rover." I threw the spear at his feet and ran into the ocean, cackling. Sometimes there's just too much of a good thing, lads.

An Afterword to this story is on page 229.

4

GET YOUR BOUCANS HERE

by
Peter Coster

'Goats. There's always goats.' Gordy Ramsay opened his eyes and glanced up at the beats licking his face. 'Go away.'

He unlashed himself from the remnants of the ship's mast then saw the footprints running towards the trees. Gordy followed, finding Stupid in a clearing.

'Oh, you'se awake. See. I saved it like you said.'

Gordy closed his eyes remembering how he'd left Stupid, real name Sid, to watch the stove, only Stupid had fallen asleep and the resulting fire had spread throughout the ship.

As the ship sank, Stupid asked what he should do so Gordy told him to save the stove. Of course Stupid was too stupid to see the sarcasm in that remark, but Gordy didn't want to ask how he'd saved a cast iron stove from a sinking ship let alone get it to shore.

'Where are we?'

'It's an island?'

'Obviously.'

'There's goats and pigs.'

'Oh great.'

'And I got the cooking grate going.'

'Anyone else here?'

'Just us.'

Gordy breathed a sigh of relief. If Black Jack Spratt learned that he, the ship's cook, had left Stupid Sid to watch the stove, resulting in the ship catching fire, he would be in a deep bowl of tripe.

'So what do we do now?' It was more a question to himself.

'You always said that if we ever got away from Black Jack we would open a restaurant.'

'A restaurant needs customers. Where are we going to find customers out here, on a deserted island?'

The funny thing was that even as Gordy asked the question, he could see that Stupid Sid wasn't as stupid as people said he was.

'You're talking about cooking *viande boucanée*. But how do we attract passing ships?'

Stupid pointed to the trees where hollow wooden tubes had been strung up by Arawak Indians who, Gordy knew, visited small islands like this to hunt. He wasn't sure why, but the wind blowing through the tubes created a sort of tune and sound carried a long way over water. Ships would come to investigate and…

'We'd better get cooking,' Gordy said, and so they began.

The meat was cut into strips and then cured over the grate. They were laced with a sauce made from marrow and rum mixed with a dash of gunpowder, and Gordy soon had a stock ready to sell. The first ship came, and it flew as they expected, the black flag of a French *flibustier*.

'*Boucans. Boucans.* Get your *boucans* here. Cooked to Gordy Ramsay's special recipe. Get your *boucans* here.'

The one thing Gordy could do was cook. He might shout and swear and curse at Sid, but Sid being stupid, didn't really care.

And so the word spread, or maybe it was the sound of the wind chimes that drew the customers in. Or maybe, the smell of fresh cooked *boucans* wafting over the Caribbean.

Whatever the case, those that flew the black flag and who found it difficult to gain supplies from legitimate outlets, headed for Gordy's island where they'd hear him call, 'Get your *boucans* here.'

(Thus the origin of the term, buccaneer.)

An Afterword to this story is on page 230.

5

A BROTHER'S KEEPER

by
Mary Agrusa

Captain Farnsworth's eyes slammed shut. Days fighting rough seas, fierce winds, and dense fog took their toll. He'd seen his crew plunge to their deaths to escape the mournful dirge that swirled in the soupy atmosphere. He'd have joined them, but his heart was already broken. Physically and emotionally spent, he retired to his cabin, took a deep drink of rum, collapsed on his bed, and passed out. He awoke to the sound of waves lapping the shore. The sun's warmth felt good through his salt encrusted damp clothes.

"It's about time you woke up!" The glare off the water blinded him. Shielding his eyes, he turned toward the sound of the voice. Standing behind him was a man dressed as a ship's captain, finely appointed. His skin was a rich caramel color, and his black hair and beard were neatly trimmed. He looked familiar, but Farnsworth was sure they'd never met. The captains he knew were white skinned and not mulatto.

"Where am I?" Farnsworth asked. "How did I get here?"

"My men found you floating in the wreckage and pulled you ashore," the stranger replied.

"My ship…."

"Gone. My men are collecting anything worth saving."

"Then all's not lost!" Farnsworth exclaimed.

"Hold on," the stranger replied, "this is my salvage operation. Any cargo of note you'd care to share?" the stranger asked. "Sort of a token of appreciation for saving your life."

"No gold or silver, if that's what you mean." The mysterious captain walked over and stood next to Farnsworth, who watched the remainder of his life plucked from the sea and out of his hands.

"I've forgotten my manners and not properly thanked you for saving my life."

His mysterious savior smiled, "Captain Sebastian Pierre at your service, sir. Let's get out of the hot sun," Sebastian said. "We'll go back to my ship. You can freshen up and have something to eat."

On the ride out to the ship, Sebastian filled Captain Farnsworth in. He'd been blown way off course in the storm. His ship ran aground off La Tortuga, home of the notorious bandit Blackbeard. Fortunately, Sebastian found Farnsworth, so he was safe. Sebastian escorted his guest to his private cabin and ordered a hot bath drawn. Opening his closet, he offered Farnsworth the pick of his wardrobe.

It felt wonderful, shedding his wet clothes. The warm water removed the salt and sand caked to his skin. Toweling off, he considered his clothing options and found a fine suit to wear. Atop a dresser lay a golden cross and chain. Farnsworth had seen one like it before. Picking it up he examined the cross. Flipping it over he saw S.D. engraved on the surface. "This can't be," he thought out loud. Rushing out to find his host, Farnsworth found Sebastian overseeing the details of a meal fit for a king.

"Where did you get this?" he demanded, waving the cross and chain in Sebastian's face.

"That was a gift from my father," Sebastian replied. His warm expression now mirrored the icy tone in his voice. "I'd appreciate you leaving my personal effects alone."

"I've seen this before," Farnsworth stammered. "My father-in-law, Captain Samuel Drake, wore one just like it."

"Then you knew my father?" Sebastian replied with wide-eyed surprise. It all made sense. Sebastian looked like Farnsworth's late wife Emily, Samuel Drake's daughter. "My condolences sir, I'd heard rumor of a half sister and her demise.

"What do you know about my wife and daughter?" Farnsworth demanded.

"A daughter you say," Sebastian replied. "I hadn't heard that. My father was a lovable scoundrel, posed as a legitimate ship's captain while acting as an *agent* for those whose wares had questionable origins. He double-crossed Blackbeard but died before revenge was administered. Rumor was his family paid the price for his foolishness."

Farnsworth collapsed into a nearby chair. "What happened to them?" he pleaded.

"I'd rather not share the fodder of gossip. Suffice to say, they didn't survive." Sebastian replied softly.

Escorted back to the cabin to rest, Farnsworth laid down. He felt the ship set sail. Through the open porthole a sorrowful wail drifted in wrapping itself around the remaining pieces of his heart and shattering them. He covered his ears to drown out the sound but to no avail.

Racing out the cabin, he crossed the deck and plunged head first into the sea. His whereabouts along with those of his wife and daughter would be substance for seafaring legends for many years to come.

An Afterword to this story is on page 231.

6

SIREN

by
Colleen Sayre

Waves crashed. She could feel the water sluicing over her body, covering her bare legs with sand and foam and detritus from the sea, but she hadn't the strength to pull herself farther up the shore. The sun had come up, and she felt surprisingly warm despite cold water lapping at her legs. *When did the sun come up?* She lay in the sand with her head on one outstretched arm, reaching for... something. The shore? Safety? No, him. She was reaching for him.

She opened salt-crusted sea-green eyes, looking through a sheet of sand-matted hair toward a mangrove thicket. Raising her throbbing head, she could see a long swath of beach and scrub but nothing more. He'd told her they were in the Abacos between two small cays, Green Turtle Cay and Scotland Cay, having glided past the uninhabited Great Guana Cay. She'd had a hard time understanding his accent, the burr thick and rum-drenched, but she knew he knew his way around these waters. He'd had the blue eyes and blond hair of the natives, the Scots who had settled these islands and lured ships into their tiny ports by lamplight to crash on the rocks. She'd seen no lights, seen nothing as they'd sailed on water like glass, seen nothing except the phosphorescence far below.

A shadow passed over her, a cloud she thought until she felt the tickle of fabric against her cheek.

"Ye'll be needin' this, lass," he said, dangling a white shirt over her head, his shirt obviously as he stood a bare-chested, swashbuckling silhouette against the sun.

"It'll protect you from sunburn. You'll no want to be lyin' there much longer letting the crabs nibble at your toes."

She struggled to sit up, grabbing the shirt as she did to cover herself.

"Storm caught you unawares, too, I see," he said. "You musta been rather busy to be caught in the buff." He grinned but turned away as she shrugged into his shirt. "You were lucky, lass, to end up here rather than out in the drink with the other poor sons-a-bitches," he said over his shoulder.

She wanted to ask, "What others?" but her throat was raw with salt and sand.

"Took a nasty rap to the head, it seems," he said turning back around. His fingers touched a tender spot over her left eye, a bump protruding on her brow. "I expect you're feeling a bit grumpy just the now, but I've a cure for that."

Handing her a bottle, he encouraged her to drink up. "It'll warm your bones," he said, "and clear your mind." She doubted that but took a swig and swallowed hard. Rum.

She looked at him with questioning eyes as he settled down in the sand.

"They say this cay's cursed, they do. Wouldn't know anythin' bout that would ye, lass?"

She shook her head, the throbbing finally letting go as the rum took hold.

"I thought not, a pretty girl like you." He smiled and winked. "Have another drink -- or two. I've another cask in the dinghy."

She perked up at the mention of a boat, green eyes flashing. "Don't get your hopes up," he said in answer to the glint in her eye. "It's a fair way to Marsh Harbor."

At that, she took his suggestion and the bloom of warmth in the pit of her belly spread. Still, her mind was foggy. She remembered only him, the one like this one, the man on the boat, the blue eyes with an urgent need. She cast another questioning look at the man sitting in the sand beside her.

"Looking for treasure, I am," he said matter-of-factly. "Been cruisin' for Old Jack's stash. My brothers an' me've scoured these isles a time or two, always washin' up on this barren stretch."

He paused and watched with silent admiration as she sat beside him, shaking sand out of long curls that gleamed gold in the sunlight. "Gold," he whispered.

She remembered.

Tossing aside the bottle of rum, she stood up to slip out of his shirt. With a smile her lips parted, and she sang the song that drove men to their knees. With one hand she reached for him. Unlike his brothers, this man was unarmed, this man who planned to steal what was hers. Holding tight, she ran to the water and dove, seeking the phosphorescence, taking him to the golden treasure that lay deep at the bottom of her sea.

An Afterword to this story is on page 232.

7

FROM THE JOURNAL OF
DELBERT THE DREAD

by
Christian Warren Freed

The most famous cutthroat and rogue, the most feared and respected, he pillaged and plundered his way across a dozen ports throughout the Caribbean. All who heard his name trembled and turned yellow. Women and riches lay at his feet in carpets of flesh and gold. There wasn't a sailor alive who didn't know the Legend of the Dreaded.

"Only that's my brother you see," Delbert said after swallowing a rather large mouthful of rum. He belched and wiped his mouth on a torn and dirty sleeve. "I don't think I've ever done a proper bit of pillaging at all!"

Thrust the Deaf sat opposite him, staring blankly and thanking God a British cannon robbed his hearing. He could tell from Delbert's posture and the movements of his mouth nothing but doom and gloom spit from between his teeth. Better not to worry about such. He plugged away at the rum before shoving it back to Delbert.

"It's always been my brother, you see. Ma always crooned about how handsome and strong he was. How determined he was to make his mark on merchant ships.

What did that leave me? Twenty doubloons and a jug of rock gut rum. Where did you get this anyway? Doesn't matter." Delbert swallowed again.

Random bits of planks and sail washed up in the tide. Delbert stared blankly at it, wondering what went wrong. They'd been sailing around the southern coast of Hispaniola when the threat of a heavy blow forced him closer to the shore. The storm never hit. It didn't have to. At first he thought he was hearing things. Beautiful voices sang across the waves. Crew flocked to the rails, desperate to find the source of the golden voices.

Delbert liked to think he was a well-grounded man. He came from a steady family, if a bit wicked, and did his best to think matters through before undertaking a task. He didn't believe in superstitious nonsense and that meant the score of women sitting on the rocks singing to them couldn't be mermaids. They couldn't.

"And now we're shipwrecked on the island of…" He paused to scratch his beard. "Well, who knows where we are exactly."

Thrust shook his head and tipped the bottle back again. At least he'd been wise enough to bring a few bottles of rum. Otherwise…

"Sometimes I envy you, Thrust," Delbert continued. "A man can bemoan his station all day, and you'd never hear it. Lucky man, you. I used to look up to my brother, but he hasn't spoken to me in years. Very dispiriting that."

Delbert took the bottle and continued to watch the waves gradually creep closer. A body bobbed on the white caps. *One Eye, I think. Maybe not. So many good men died last night. What kind of captain was I? A bloody failure at best.*

Once again his thoughts strayed to his brother, the dashing villain that he was. Women swooned at his charm, muscles, and easy manner. He was the kind of captain that made others want to follow him without question. Delbert once fell under that spell. His brother could do no wrong in his clouded eyes. But the veil was gone. Reality set in. His brother disappeared into his own work, leaving Delbert's name a stain on their family honor.

He took another drink. "You see, the problem with this world is that very few folks want to help another man, especially one in need. Take that fella that gave me the map in the first place. He swore we'd be fine and that the treasure at the end of the path was worth the risk. Bah! Look where that got us—shipwrecked and nearly dead to the man. You just can't trust anyone, Thrust. I swear."

The older man shook his head and lay down in the sand. Their tiny fire warmed them enough that he was fast asleep in minutes. Delbert looked down on him with admiration. He didn't know how anyone could sleep after what they went through, but Thrust was a true professional. Delbert finally realized that the hero types didn't need to be admired. It was the common man who did the most, earned the most. Satisfied with his revelation, Delbert put his head down on a pile of rags and drifted asleep.

Getting off the island was another issue and could wait until morning.

An Afterword to this story is on page 233.

8

THE MYSTERIOUS ISLAND

by
Scott Amis

Davis Wilson came to consciousness at a nudge to his ribs. A man in military camouflage offered him a hand, and he pulled himself up. Beyond the white beach the ocean stretched to the horizon.

"Wh... where am I?"

"On an island somewhere. I just now found you."

"Am I the only one?"

"So far as I can see."

"No signs of a sail yacht?"

The stranger shook his head. "Nothing at all. Come on, mate. I'll get you dry clothes."

Davis followed the man across a hundred feet of beach and into a jungle. A large shack built from the wreckage of boats stood in a clearing. The man opened a door. "This is my bush hut. Keeps the rain out." He took military fatigues and boots from a chest. "Wash up in the freshwater spring outside and put these on. I'll make us some food."

Davis returned to the shack and took a seat. The stranger served hot bowls of canned stew and raised an eyebrow. "What happened?"

Davis put his head in his hands. "Last night my sailboat hit a reef that wasn't on the charts. It tore the hull open from bow to stern, and the boat sank in seconds. My wife and daughters and five crewmen were on board with me."

"Sorry I couldn't help you more, mate. Like some rum?"

"I would." Davis drained the tin cup and felt better. "Can I ask what you're doing here?"

"Sure. My navy patrol boat hit the same reef ten years ago. Me and a coupla mates made it here in a lifeboat."

"They've since passed away?"

"I ate them."

Davis dropped his spoon. "Huh?"

The stranger grinned and pointed an auto pistol at him. "That reef keeps me in supplies and fresh meat. You'd be next on the menu, but I see you've got a nice trinket on your wrist."

"My watch?" Davis looked at his platinum Rolex.

The stranger jerked the pistol. Davis got up, and the man pushed him into the clearing. He pointed at a range of low mountains that rose at the far edge of the jungle, a mile away. "Here's the deal. I give you an hour head start for your watch. If you outrun me and make it to the other side of the mountains, you're home free."

"What's on the other side?"

"No idea. I've never bothered to climb them."

Davis gave him the watch. "Looks like I've no other option."

The stranger pointed the pistol at his head and handed him a machete. "Right on that, mate. Better get moving."

Davis dodged snakes and spiders as he hacked through dense jungle growth. He paused for a breath. His heart ached with anguish for his wife and daughters. And he, an M.D. and tech whiz who'd sold his medical software company for a billion at fifty and retired to sail the seas, was now in the same predicament as the unlucky soul in a short story he'd read as a boy. He put his grief and recriminations aside and pushed into the jungle ahead.

The mountain slope was far less steep than he'd expected, and he took to it at a run. Halfway up, he looked behind. No sign of the stranger. He picked up pace and in a mighty effort climbed over the ridge at the mountaintop. More jungle lay below but he had outrun the stranger and kept his life.

He crept forward with caution. Dry wood snapped and he raised the machete. Four aborigines sprang from behind trees, flint-tipped spears trained on him. The stranger stepped from behind them and stood with hands on his waist. "You made it."

"You said you'd never climbed the mountains."

"You believed a jerk like me?"

"I had no choice."

"You didn't, and that's sad. All of that sweat and you're still going to be dinner." He glanced at the aborigines. "I have a deal with these blokes. I catch the meat, and they smoke it. Then we all sit down to a feast."

Davis lunged and swung the machete at the stranger's neck. Blood spurted as he gurgled and dropped to his knees. Davis grabbed the pistol from his belt and pointed it at the aborigines. They lowered their spears and drew back.

Davis took his watch from the body and nodded to the aborigines. "He's all yours. Enjoy your meal."

He turned and plunged back toward the mountain. The stranger's hideout was his now, and he began to wonder what smoked people might taste like.

An Afterword to this story is on page 234.

CALL OF THE SIRENS

by
Arlene Lagos

Water fills my lungs as I plunge farther down into the frozen waters. The shore is but a few hundred yards, but I am no swimmer. Accepting my fate, I stop kicking and let it take me to my watery grave.

Suddenly, I feel something wrap around my waist, then hands, then a huge tug. My head rips through the top of the water, and I'm dangling from a human fishing pole several feet in the air. Beside me floating in the tide is a ship.

"Not much o' a swimmer be you?" a man calls out.

Blinking the water out of my eyes, I focus on his face. He's tall, muscular with dark black hair that flows sweetly in the sun. Covered in tattoos and armed with a sword, I knew right away he was a jack tar.

"You saved my life," I gasp, coughing water out of my lungs.

"It would be rude o' me t' let a vixen like you wind up in Davey Jones' locker."

Pulling the rope towards the boat, he lowers me gently onto the ship, and then puts out his hand.

"Name's Marcus. This be me ship and that man thar,

climbin' up t' boat is me mate, Angus."

Slowly spinning me around, he stops, then points to the island behind me.

"And that starboard thar be our island."

"You're island? Impressive."

"That's right. Just me and me bucko Angus livin' off t' spoils o' this place since t' rest o' t' crew went t' Davey Jones' locker when t' second ship capsized."

"How awful. So you are here all alone? Just the two of you?" I asked.

"Aye, just t' two o' us. So, little lady, what might be yer name and what you be doin' out here, bravin' these waters?"

"My name is Anna. I'm a scientist. My crew and I were on an expedition to find raw materials, when we heard this enchanting music. It drew us right in, like we had no say in the matter."

"Ah aye, t' siren's call. Always drawin' men in and sinkin' their ships just before they reach shore. Them beauties be devils."

"I don't remember seeing this island on any of my maps," I said.

"No you won't find this island on any map. It be t' secret island o' lost mates. Years ago all t' rum runners, treaaye hunters, and jack tars o' t' high seas stored their riches here. Now it's just me and Angus port t' inherit it all."

Leaning in closely, pressing his body against mine, he whispered in my ear.

"Nobody will ever find ya here. It will be nice t' have a beauty around t' keep me warm at night."

Playing along, I slide my hand down the small of his back until I feel the bottom of a revolver buried in the belt of his pants. As he continues to kiss my neck, I don't move, but my eyes follow Angus as he strolls away towards the other side of the ship.

A gun goes off. Marcus pulls away at the sound, just in time for me to relieve him of his weapon.

"What was that?" he reaches for his gun.

"Looking for this?"

I point the gun at his head and watch as Serena appears on the aft of the boat.

"The fat man's dead," she said.

"Who be you, Anna?" asks Marcus.

"Actually, you might know me better as Avielle, Queen of the Sirens."

Eyes wide, Marcus gasps.

"I can see by the look in your eyes that my reputation precedes me."

"I thought you were just a legend... a ghost story made up by other jack tars t' keep us away from the island. No, you can't be real!"

Pulling back his arm, I lean in and stick the gun to his side.

"Does this gun feel real enough to you?"

"What be my fate here?" he asks.

Leaning in again even closer this time, my lips speak softly into his ear.

"Me and t' lass will be takin' your ship, your island, and your treaayes... and maybe if you're a real good lad, I'll let live."

With his hands now behind his back, I tie off the rope, leaving him to sit as Serena approaches.

"Serena, call the other sirens, let them know that it's safe to come back home... and that I have a present for them."

An Afterword to this story is on page 235.

THE HONEYMOONERS

by
Harry Alexiou

"Wake up Ginny! Please wake up!"

Ricardo slapped her face, but she didn't respond. His arms were heavy and burning with fatigue after bringing her to shore following the sinking. He ignored the cramp in his legs. "Come on! Come back to me!" he screamed as he frantically attempted to resuscitate his wife of only three days. He broke down sobbing and dropped his head to her lifeless body. No heartbeat could be heard within. The ocean had filled her lungs and mercilessly replaced vital oxygen with water. Ricardo knew before they'd reached the white sandy shoreline she'd been cruelly taken from him. Now he was alone. The honeymoon Caribbean cruise of a lifetime had become the cruise from hell.

"She's gone," said a quiet voice. "I will help you bury her."

Ricardo opened his eyes and raised his head, not sure if he'd imagined it. He twisted around sharply as he stood and came face to face with a shoeless, dark-skinned man dressed in white t-shirt and badly cropped jeans. In one hand he held a bottle, containing clear liquid, which he raised up toward Ricardo. Ricardo stood, scared and confused. He looked around the shoreline and out to sea before looking back at the man.

"Who are you?"

"Who am I? I should ask you the same question." He lowered the unclaimed bottle and looked down at the body. "Sorry for your loss."

Ricardo wiped his face dry and backed away from the stranger, noticing the knife clipped on his belt.

"You have nothing to fear from me, my friend, for you have lost everything, it seems. We must bury her now"

Ricardo was numb as he grabbed Ginny's arms and lifted her from the sand. The stranger lifted her legs, but as he did so Ricardo lost his grip and dropped his wife to the sand. Ginny coughed violently, and the stranger quickly turned her to one side as seawater spilled from her mouth. She continued coughing as Ricardo knelt down beside her. His tears, now of joy, flowed freely as he embraced his wife. The dark stranger walked away along the shoreline and proceeded to pick up selected washed up items, leaving the couple to reacquaint.

"What happened, Hun?" Ginny asked, holding her head. "Who's he?"

"The ship capsized... I swam you here after you'd hit your head and fell unconscious."

"But all the other passengers... are they dead?"

"I don't know, Ginny. The only other person I've seen is him," he said, fixing his stare on the man, now quite some distance from them. "He appeared out of nowhere. We should make a move inland to find shelter. It'll be dark soon." He stood and helped his wife to her feet. Both had their backs to the stranger as they dusted off the sand.

"Leaving so soon?" the voice asked.

"What? How the…" Ricardo's startled gaze shifted to a bulging wallet in the strangers hand.

"Before you run off into the jungle," he interrupted, "allow me to formally introduce myself. My name is Gerald, and this is my home. I like to think of myself as a modern day Robin Hood. There is much wealth weaving in and out of these islands every day. Some seafarers succumb to the changeable weather in seasonal stormy seas, and others carelessly leave their riches unattended whilst dipping in the many lagoons.

"I don't get it. What's the point of robbing the rich and collecting all this stuff?" said Ricardo extending his hand to the shoreline, "You live on a deserted island, Gerald."

"Yes, I admit it seems odd," replied Gerald as he nestled down in the sand. "Let me explain. My home was in Haiti. The devastating earthquake of January 2010 left me with no family and no home, and I wept for days after, but the suffering of those still living spurred me on to help. The months which followed were… difficult." He raised his head high and continued. "Whatever I collect I divide among the neediest, and there are still so many whom I have yet to assist." The honeymooners sat down in the sand flabbergasted by the revelation from Gerald, a man who Ricardo had ill-judged.

"Gerald," began Ricardo, "I really admire what you're doing, and I'm sorry for your loss." The sound of helicopter blades thumping in the distance caused the honeymooners to look skyward. They rushed to the water's edge frantically waving and screaming. They hugged and turned back to Gerald.

"Gerald?"

The hollow in the sand where he'd sat was the only evidence of his existence. They agreed to keep it that way.

An Afterword to this story is on page 236.

LUCIA

by
Joyce Shaughnessy

The ship I had worked on had run aground onto a large boulder. It was a huge yacht, with fourteen employees to take care of one very spoiled heiress who didn't even appreciate the beauty of the ocean as she lounged on the deck. She wore expensive jewelry and lay upon her cushioned chaise with her sunglasses and large hat. She didn't seem satisfied by the luxury of the ship or the beauty of the ocean. She spat invectives at her employees, who met her every need and command. When the ship fell apart, I managed to grab onto a board and paddle for two days before I found this little secluded island and succeeded in dragging my limp body onto the sand where I rested for a few hours.

Sometimes I could sense a presence behind me. I would quickly look behind me, but there was never anyone there. Sometimes when I went into the jungle in search of food, I would find faint footprints in the dirt, but I knew that I hadn't walked along this path in days. I looked and looked, hoping to find someone, anyone. I was terribly lonely and feeling desperate, afraid that I would be alone for the rest of my life, existing on coconuts and berries. The island provided only the barest necessities of life. I kept track of the days I had been on the island with a calendar of sorts I had fashioned in the dirt in a protected little cave I had found.

I was able to create a crude abode in the cave, but in the fourth week on the island I found faint footprints in the sand, smaller than my own. They weren't made by a wild animal - that much I could tell. A few days later, I found a beautiful jeweled ring nestled in one of the rocks that I had been using for shelter against the elements. That puzzled me more than anything. The tide couldn't have brought the ring in because the rock was protected from it. *Could a monkey have found it and hidden it here?* That was the only rational explanation, but sometimes logic escaped me. I was starting to get goose bumps when I thought of the footprints and the ring. The feeling that I was being watched by a human never left me.

One day I found a letter opener and a pair of reading glasses. That was when I was certain there was someone watching me. I decided to stay inside the cave, hoping to catch the other person red-handed.

I waited for days, but it drained my energy. I couldn't hunt for food any longer, and I had nothing to drink but water from the small pond just outside the cave, which sometimes had a foul taste to it. I soon forgot to mark the days and nights as they passed, and I became confused over how long I had been in the cave. But, finally, I heard the voice of another person.

She softly asked me, "What is your name? Mine is Lucia." She had long dark hair which shined in the moonlight.

"My name is Henry. How long have you been on this island, and how did you end up here?"

"I was on a ship as a cook's mate. We were boarded by drug smugglers, I think. I managed to escape. They killed the rest of the crew. It's been about two years. I've been watching you, wondering how you would react to me. I don't need anyone other than a friend, and I'm wary of strangers. This is the first time I've spoken to another person in all this time."

"Why did you leave the ring and the letter opener?"

"They were the only real possessions I owned. They washed up on shore with me. I wanted to share them with someone – a friend."

"Lucia, I hope you will let me be that friend. I promise not to hurt you. You've been hurt enough. We need to depend on one another. I'm afraid I don't own anything of value. I couldn't salvage anything. Where do you live?"

"On the other side of the island. There's a small cove there and even a fresh water pond. You can come live there with me – that is if I can trust you."

"Who else can you trust?" I reached into the cave for her treasures and then took her hand. I put the ring on her finger and carried the opener and reading glasses.

"Let's see what we can find together on your side of the island."

An Afterword to this story is on page 237.

12

MERGERS & AQUISITIONS

by
Gail Harkins

The music of a steel drum band was barely audible over the crash of waves on the reef as the small catamaran approached the channel. Connor perked up immediately.

"You didn't say there's a party!"

"There's not," his wife replied. "Help me spot the opening." She scanned the waves, eventually spying the gap. "Prepare to come about!"

Connor readied the winch to haul the boom around.

"Coming about!" She turned the tiller.

"What do you mean 'no party'?! I'm stuck here with you?" he shouted, letting the line slacken.

"Connor!"

From the jungle, a man watched the wind spill from the sail and saw a pontoon rise as it scrapped the coral. The boat, taking on water, limped to shore, but he remained in the shadows, watching. He heard the couple clearly, as they inspected the damage.

"This wasn't how I wanted to spend today!" Connor complained. "I could've lunched with Martin Albrecht."

Suddenly attentive, the watcher focused binoculars on Connor, dismissed him, and then sought the woman. Her emerald-green bikini accentuated an inviting figure. She brushed wavy hair from her face and smiled despite the situation. She was worthy of attention.

"The corporate raider? He made millions dismantling companies." Her eyes flashed. "Is that why we're in the Caribbean? I thought you craved romance... After all, this is our first anniversary!"

Connor scowled, and she changed tack. "This could be very romantic... stranded on an island, a loaf of bread, a jug of wine, and thou or, in our case, lobster, baguettes, strawberries and champagne..."

"Strawberries give me hives!" Connor huffed, carrying the picnic basket higher onto the beach. "What I wouldn't give for a beer!"

The observer stepped from the trees, dangling an unopened Heineken between two fingers. "A better question, I think, is what you would give for a beer."

Connor rocked back on his heels. "Where'd you come from? Can you get us off this piece of..."

"Island," Lori interjected, introducing herself and her husband.

"Call me Marty." His gray eyes were kind, and his smile inviting.

When he turned to Connor, however, he arched one eyebrow questionably, and glanced toward Lori. When Connor shrugged, Marty changed tactics.

"You're trespassing. Reparations must be made." This time, he addressed his silent question directly to Lori. The corners of her mouth turned up ever so slightly.

"Hey! We're below the high tide line," Connor complained. "Maritime law states..."

"You're on dry land," Marty countered, pulling a .45 from the back of his jeans.

Connor rounded on Lori. "This is your fault!" he hissed. "If you hadn't insisted on sailing, I could've contacted Albrecht. I'd be rich, and everything would be fine. But no, you wanted time, you wanted romance. You've ruined everything."

"You made us hit the reef, and you don't even know Albrecht," Lori pointed out calmly.

"Enough!" Marty leveled the pistol at Connor. "Payment."

"All...all right," Connor stammered. "You take checks?" He reached for his wallet.

"No. Your wife." Marty glanced at Lori, gauging her reaction. She tensed, but didn't protest.

Connor considered. "Yeah. Okay. You can have her...but no returns!" He glared at Lori, whose eyes widened in disbelief.

Marty nodded thoughtfully. He tossed Connor the beer. "My boat will return you to the resort tonight." He addressed Lori. "Do you want to stay the course—" he extended his hand "—or are you ready for a new heading?"

Defiantly, she grabbed the picnic basket and accepted his hand. When they entered the jungle, she didn't look back.

The dappled light was a welcome contrast to the glare of the beach. As they walked, her anger was replaced with shock. Cavalierly discarded by her husband and claimed by a stranger... How could she have allowed that?!

"Who are you?" she finally asked.

"Apparently, a corrupting influence," he laughed. "Would you rather go back?"

She stopped, pulling him to face her. "Why should I go with you?"

"Where's your sense of adventure? Shipwrecked, whisked away by a handsome stranger..."

She laughed. "You've flair, I'll give you that."

Later, as the stars came out, they sat on the rose-colored terrace of a villa at the back of the cay, watching the lights of a speedboat making for the largest of the distant islands. Steel drums softly played.

"Don't be sad. He wasn't worthy of you." Marty touched her hand gently.

She fingered the monogram on his shirt. "M-N-A. Mergers and acquisitions?" she teased.

His eyes twinkled. "Sort of. Martin Nathanial Albrecht."

An Afterword to this story is on page 238.

13

A MOUSER, A KEG OF RUM, & A GUNNERY MATE

by
Randall Lemon

Jamie Fotheringay had been serving aboard a British privateer in the Caribbean for one year. Their mission had been to try to disrupt the flow of gold from the New World back to Spain. They had been moderately successful in this endeavor. In their last encounter with the treasure fleet, Jamie's ship, *The Reliant* had taken heavy damage to its mast and had barely managed to withdraw without being sunk. They sailed northeasterly somewhere between Bermuda and the land known as Florida. They were seeking an island with a harbor and plenty of trees they could use to repair the mast. Suddenly out of a clear blue sky, a fearsome storm came upon them, and soon The Reliant lay somewhere beneath the sea. Jamie had awoken to find himself cast up on a beach as black as midnight at sea.

Jamie walked the beach looking for companions or anything that might have washed up from his ship. Scattered at various places he found items from his ship and other less familiar ones that might have washed up from other wrecks. One particularly lucky find was an untapped cask of rum. Nearby the cask lay a belaying pin and when he picked up the pin, a small crab scuttled away revealing a bosun's whistle. He cleared the tube of sand and gave it an experimental blow. The crisp clear call of the whistle sounded even above the crashing of waves.

As if in answer, a piercing scream came from the jungle. Not knowing if it was a person or some fearsome jungle beast, Jamie hefted the belaying pin and moved off the shore and into the dense greenery. He turned as the sound of something moving through the underbrush toward him reached his ears. He held the pin and prepared to use it as a club to defend himself from whatever monstrous creature sprang at him.

Suddenly with a flash of gray fur, the beast hurled himself at Jamie, jumping for his leg. Startled at first, Jamie laughed with relief when he realized that the fearsome beast was his ship's cat, Jiggs.

"Ah, Jiggs! How did you wind up here? Cats can't swim. Did you hitch a ride here with someone else?" It was then Jamie noticed the blood on Jiggs' front paws. "What have you been into, Jiggs? Did you catch an island rat?" He picked Jiggs up and ruffled his fur and set off to find Jiggs' companions. And find him he did. On the far side of the island lay a wrecked dinghy. It had been smashed against some rocks and lay splintered and useless. Not far from it lay the body of young Ensign Aames, who appeared to have absorbed as much damage as the dinghy. When the ship started going down, Aames had probably grabbed Jiggs and made it to the boat only to wind up dead, broken on the rocky shore.

Now there was nothin' to do but bury the lad. Once he had placed Aames in his final resting place, Jamie used the whistle to pipe Aames to his final rest.

Just then Jamie noticed a ship rounding the curve in the island. Shielding his eyes against the sun, he could make out the flag on its mizzenmast. It bore the distinctive jolly roger of Calico Jack Rackham.

Jamie had seen Rackham once before in a Port Royal inn and knew that the captain could be an amiable gentleman or the devil himself, depending on his mood. Jamie waited on the beach, stroking Jiggs' ears while a long boat approached shore bearing Calico Jack himself.

As he stepped out of the boat, Calico squinted at Jamie and his furry companion. "I be knowin' you, don't I?"

"Indeed you do Captain. Jamie Fotheringay, late gunnery mate aboard *The Reliant*, Sir."

"Where be your ship? We didn't see one as we approached."

"She and the rest of the crew minus the poor boy I buried here sit in Davey Jones' locker. Jiggs here and I are all that's left of *The Reliant* now, that and a keg of rum I have back at my camp."

"Is your Jiggs there a good mouser?"

"The best there be." Jamie replied.

Rackham sized Jamie up for a moment. "A mouser, a keg of rum, and a gunnery mate! Looks like you have ideal credentials to be joining the crew of *The Kingston*. Unless of course you would rather stay here and wait for the Selkies to get you?"

An Afterword to this story is on page 239.

14

ESCAPING CAPTAIN DRAKE

by
H. M. Schuldt

Pearl watched the tip of her boat go down. If only he would have listened, they wouldn't be stuck on an island with a bunch of nutcase inmates. Josh had to get as close as he could to see the prison, but it wasn't the building that drew him in. Something else had captured his attention, and Pearl was enraged.

She cried out in disappointment. "Don't you know how to drive a boat?" She yelled over the waves that were crashing down around Josh. She was young and so was he. Her blood boiled with uncontrollable anger, an outburst that would make any animal yield to her command. "You just had to get close to the prison island! Well, how's this for close? You happy now?"

Josh stepped away from the waves, barefoot on the sand, away from Pearl in her crazy fit. He stopped and turned his head toward a melody, almost in a bizarre trance, in the direction of a pier. "There it is again. Listen."

Pearl shouted, using her strong pop star voice. "What kind of crazy lady would sing to the ocean? She must be crazy just like you!"

Suddenly he snapped back to Pearl's conversation. "What kind of crazy lady would travel all over the world and sing for millions of people?" Josh spoke about Pearl. He had been her manager, her booking agent, her everything, and he had been the one who paved her way to success.

"Oh, you'll be begging for my help, princess, but I won't be around anymore because you're fired!" Josh said.

"What? You can't fire me! I'm the one who sings and makes money. You never scheduled Vegas like I told you to, so you're fired!"

And so the young lovers went. The effect he had on her was indescribable, a young love relationship built on hidden grenades. Her foolish reasoning led her to believe she didn't need him on this terrible island. She turned away in revulsion to go find some real help.

For miles in both directions, the shore stretched with hot burning sand. Josh and Pearl walked in opposite directions, each one convinced *they* would be the one to save the other.

Pearl walked as far as she could until she arrived where loud waves crashed on top of boulders. A monstrous rock-wall consisting of one shallow cave caught her attention. It blocked her way and forced her to look up. She saw a person sitting up on a lonely edge. He looked as though he might be in confinement. Her eyes widened when she recognized it was a missing CIA agent who had been all over the news, Arnie Walker.

It took quite some time to climb up the rocks. Pulling herself up, she drew as near as she could possibly get. First she asked him why he was up there. Next she asked him how to get off the island, and Arnie happened to know. He warned her about Captain Drake, nicknamed *El Draco*, who takes inmates as a crew on his ship, the *Golden Hind*. After a short discussion, she quickly agreed to go find a rum maker who could get her off the island and how to get Arnie down off the wall.

Finally, she found the warehouse. Arnie had given her good directions.

Pearl saw the rum maker, Rack, driving a forklift. She flagged him down and impatiently waited for him to shut off the engine. As usual, Pearl went right to the point, knowing exactly what she needed, but Rack didn't seem like he was going to cooperate about getting Arnie down.

"You can't leave Arnie out there. He'll starve." Pearl was appalled.

"People go fer days without eatin' nothin'. It's part of El Draco's Fellowship," Rack said. "No matter fer you, missy. Arnie's life is gone. He's been sent to the *Golden Hind*. He's better off up there than down here with El Draco itchin' to get back out to sea. Where ye come from?"

"The name's Pearl. My boat went down, and I had to swim to shore with… my manager."

"Jus' you and him?"

Pearl nodded. "Yeah, so?"

"Ye better leave first thing in the mornin'. A supply ship sails out at noon." Rack was in a hurry to get back to work. "It's the only safe way to get off the island."

Pearl called out. "Hey! Where are we supposed to stay the night around here?"

"You and yer manager can stay in my cabin fer jus' one night. Stay in after dark. Whatever you do, don't go down to the pier."

"Why not?" Pearl asked.

"It's cursed with the ghost of Bonny O'Baily. She was a sea captain who stole the hearts of sailors with her singin' and dancin', and she left 'em with nothin'. She'll take yer soul if ye get too close, and you'll live forever in Davey Jones' locker. Better stay away from the pier!"

On the other side of the island, Josh found something useful. Almost at the same time, Pearl and Josh returned to the place where they last saw each other, both feeling overly confident, both expecting the other one to apologize, both convinced they hadn't done anything wrong.

Josh held out a cast iron pan, feeling proud of his discovery. "Did you find anything we can use?"

Pearl spoke arrogantly. "Iguana eggs, rum, and... a supply boat that leaves tomorrow. I even found a cabin where we can stay the night."

"I met some guy, Diego, with one eye. He gave me this pan and said he's leaving in the morning," Josh said.

"Can you make a fire?" Pearl asked.

"Piece of cake. I'll tell you what. I'll make scrambled eggs, if you take me to the rum."

"Deal."

The next day, Pearl and Josh were sailing away when they realized that they were with Arnie, one-eyed Diego, and Captain Drake on the flagship, the *Golden Hind*.

An Afterword to this story is on page 240.

15

RECRUITED

by
Lynette White

Garth was asleep in his cabin under the quarterdeck when they hit the rocks. By the time the Sailing Master stumbled out to see what was happening, the hull was torn open from the figurehead to mid-ship.

He rushed back into his cabin and stuffed his most crucial instruments, a dagger and what money he had, into an oilcloth bag. Most of his men were dead by the time Garth jumped over the side of the sinking ship.

He grabbed a board to keep afloat and started to swim toward the island. The last thing he remembered was the explosion of pain in his head as a piece of debris struck him from behind.

"Sailing Master, can you hear me? Please wake up, Master," an anxious voice pleaded.

Garth groaned at the sound of the rigger's voice. It was the dry rumbling voice of the one man who annoyed him to death. Seth never stopped talking.

Now I know the gods hate me if Seth and I are the only survivors, Garth lamented silently.

Garth squeezed his eyes closed. He knew his skin was burning, but his lungs were too. Hot sand spread on his bare back, and the heat warned him that he had to move off the beach. The sun was suddenly blocked out, so he forced his eyes open. Even with Seth standing over him, Garth's eyes burned, so he raised his hand as a shield.

"Oh, thank the gods you are alright, Master." Seth rejoiced and dropped to his knees next to Garth. "Are you hurt?"

"Shut up, Seth!" Garth snapped, closing his eyes again.

"But, Master, you have to get off the beach. You are burning up out here. I have found shade and fresh water. I even have a little bit of food I was able to salvage from the wreckage." Seth insisted.

The Sailing Master opened his eyes and tried to sit up. The rigger placed a hand on his back to support him.

"I am fine, Seth." Garth growled. "Just give me a minute."

The Sailing Master forced himself to his feet. Seth helped him find his bag then escorted him to the shaded area. Garth rested while Seth foraged for more food, firewood, and materials to build a shelter.

They just started to eat their dinner when they heard someone approaching the camp. It was too late to extinguish the fire, so Garth grabbed his dagger and positioned himself in the shadows.

Moments later a stranger strolled into their camp dressed in a green tunic, brown pants, and high brown boots. Before the intruder could defend himself, Garth had the stranger's arm pulled back, holding a dagger at his throat.

"Now, now, my good man. Is this the way to treat someone who is here to help you?" asked the stranger. He cautiously patted a canister hanging from his hip. "I even have some rum to share."

Garth lowered his dagger and shoved the stranger toward the fire. "Who are you? What island is this?"

The stranger paused to straighten his clothes. "The name is Courtney Agmire, and you are on Blackman Isle." He introduced himself with a slight bow.

"And your name, good sir?" Courtney asked.

"Garth McGanie, Sailing Master of the *Red Swan*. Did you say we're on Blackman Isle?"

Courtney's eyebrows went up. "You're a Sailing Master? The captain will be most pleased. His last navigator suffered an untimely death." He wagged his head ruefully. "Most unfortunate time to misread his maps." He turned to Seth. "And your name?"

Seth swallowed hard. "Seth McFarsen, sir."

"And what did *you* do on the *Red Swan*?"

"Outside of being an annoying boil on my back," Garth answered for him, "he is the best rigger in the business."

Courtney laughed. "Indeed! Then I have fortunate news for both of you. The captain will most likely press you into his service instead of selling you at the slave auction. Sorry about your ship, but you were too close to the shore to suit the captain."

Seth gasped. "The singing we heard."

Garth turned his attention to the rigger. "The what?"

Courtney cleared his throat. "Well, Angelica is the captain's wife. She has unique powers. She uses them to bewitch the seaman at the helm of the intruding ship."

Now Garth was furious. "So that witch intentionally wrecked my ship? Who is this captain?"

Courtney straightened up to his full height. "Why, Captain Blackman of course, the most feared pirate in the entire Caribbean."

Garth groaned and dropped down on the log. "Oh, gods! Captain Blackman! Now I do need a drink."

An Afterword to this story is on page 241.

16

THE SCARLETT PRIMUS

by
Sylvia Stein

Journal: Day 22

December 29, 2005

It has been 22 days since our ship left the coast of the Caribbean. It sank half way down into shaky waters during a violent storm. Now we find ourselves surrounded by Arm Bandits that are awaiting our every move. I have no idea what is going to be of our fate. I just hope that I am able to figure out what I can do for my crew. I am the Captain of The Scarlett Primus, and I will protect my seamen until the end.

Captain Shane Hillstrand

Those were the last words written in his dusty journal that was found a few months after his ship had been reported missing. My name is Leo Hillstrand, and my father was Captain Shane Hillstrand. Ever since I can remember, he spoke frequently about his love for the sea. I can still recall him teaching me, when I was a young child, all the ropes surrounding his ship, and he told me how much fun it would be to sail together.

"Now Leo," he said firmly when I was young, "the sea can be a beautiful place, but it can also be a giant storm. It's an important job to know how to navigate the waters." His words echoed as a memory, ringing through me as I looked into one of the empty cabins.

As I walked on the abandoned ship, I could imagine his deck hands and seamen preparing for their next trip. I could not help but wonder what had gone so wrong. Part of me did not want to accept that all the men including their own captain had not survived. I was very close to my father in spite of the fact he spent most of the time at sea. Captain Shane Hillstrand always made sure he spent the most time he could with his beloved wife, Scarlett.

I can still recall when he named his ship. "There is only one name that I have always wanted and that is *Scarlett* like your mother. But I do want to also acknowledge my Scottish heritage, so I will combine it with the word *Primus*, which means *first*."

I continued walking through half of the ship above water, looking for clues that could tell me what happened to my father and his crew. Suddenly, I was captured by an enticing musical sound. The music faded in and out as I walked closer to the sunken half of the ship. It was like there was some type of curse that lingered in the air, and the melody was telling me something.

The faint music made me drift back into a pleasant memory, when I had graduated from high school. At that time, I had decided to embark on a new journey alongside my father. But he knew of the hardships at sea, and he decided he did not want me to have to face such risky endeavors. My father wanted me to stay on land. Therefore, in order to please him, I decided to become a doctor of Internal Medicine. It was a fond memory when I was in my last year of residency. Both of my parents could not be more proud. Then all at once, I had an unfamiliar vision of him toasting with his shipmates on *The Scarlett Primus.*

As a coast guard was helping with the search, I tried to stay hopeful that we would find him and his crew.

"Have we searched all the premises?" I asked nervously.

"Well, I am sorry to tell you this," said the head of the coast guard. "My men have searched this island and there is no sign of anyone. Considering the condition of the ship, they must of have fallen underwater."

His words made me feel helpless. "Okay, well, I need to gather the remainder of his belongings and then… call my mother and let her know."

"Take your time," he said.

But it was impossible to believe he was gone. I couldn't accept that my father and his crew had not survived the violent storm. In his last journal entry, he stated:

The Arm Bandits were awaiting us.

Then my thoughts shifted towards my mother. *How is she going to take this news? There is a rough road ahead.* I held tight onto the journal that he kept. On the front cover, my father wrote,

Captain Shane Hillstrand

Before I walked out of what was left of *The Scarlett*

Primus, the faint music came back, and I had another vision of my father and his crew taking a sip of rum, assuring each other that they would find a way to survive. That's when I knew that they, along with their ship, would be back again.

An Afterword to this story is on page 242.

17

OFF TO THE SEAS

by
Janet Bond

Jack loves being in charge. When he said, "Susie, we're going on a trip to the Caribbean," I said, "Bring it on! I'm ready for anything!"

It was an early Saturday morning. Jack and I were excited to get to sea. We found our ship, the *Deep Red Sea*. It didn't look like the cruise ship I was expecting. It was a sailing ship with three masts. I looked questioningly at Jack, and he smiled back at me.

We put our belongings in a small cabin and quickly found the bar. I ordered dark rum to help me relax, but the bartender gave me the whole bottle. Jack went to check on his valuables back in our room, so I had another drink.

That's when I saw him—a strange looking young boy with a patch over his eye. He had a sword in his hand and was swinging it like he was trying to cut someone.

"Hey, little boy," I called to him. "You'd better be careful."

Instead of answering me with words, he made the most awful looking face and acted like he was going to slash me.

Then Jack came back, bringing four other people with him. I was about to point out the boy with the sword when I noticed he was gone.

Jack said, "These are the rest of the passengers." We all felt the ship start to rock. "Off we go mates!"

The bartender poured us all another drink and then pointed up at the white flag with a skull on it waving back and forth on the highest mast. "To the dead man's ship," he said and then downed his drink.

After dinner I was resting in my cabin when I first heard the music. It sounded ancient, an old tune playing on old instruments. I went on deck to find out where it was coming from, but no one was there. The moon was high in the sky, and the music seemed to hover over the water.

The music was replaced with a loud scraping sound. I stumbled and hit my head on something. The deck was spinning, and I was afraid. It felt like the ship was tossing, breaking in half, and pulling apart.

I woke up lying on the sand of an island. "Jack! Jack!" I called over and over. I looked up and down the beach and only saw pieces of the ship floating in the waves. So I sat down on a rock, not knowing what else to do. That's when I saw him—the young boy with the sword.

"Where is the crew?" I cried.

"They be dead and sinking t' Davey Jones' locker." His voice startled me. It wasn't the voice of a boy, but of an old man, raspy and dry.

"Not my friend, Jack!" I cried. Tears began to roll down my face.

The boy held out his hand to me. "Come with me, lass. I be not hurting ye, but we must be leavin'."

I tried to put my hand in his. I saw it, but I couldn't feel his flesh. It made me pull away.

"I know ye be frightened lass. Me name be Jimmy and I got a sad story t' tell ye."

Somehow I knew he wasn't going to hurt me, so I let him lead me on a walk.

"I tried t' scare ye off that cursed boat, but ye wouldn't leave. 'Twas a cursed boat. They flew th' dead man's colors, thinkin' it fun for th' tourists, but they called down a curse on themselves and now they all be drowned. Them not be the first to add their treasures t' my gold that lay under the waves, and they not be th' last."

Jimmy led me through the jungle. We talked about treasure and sailing and good rum. Near dawn I saw a light through the trees. Then I heard Jack's voice calling to me. I ran to him, and thew my arms around him.

"Jimmy saved me," I said.

"Who's Jimmy?" Jack asked.

"The boy who helped me. He's right over..." I said, pointing back down the trail, but Jimmy was gone.

Jack put his arm around me and walked me to the beach and the rescue boats. He patted me on the head like I was a kid. "Don't worry, Susie. I've got everything under control."

But I knew better. I nodded and said, "Thank you," to Captain Jimmy.

An Afterword to this story is on page 243.

18

JACKIE & THE
DEVIL'S DOUBLOON

by
Alli Vaughan

"Yeh smell as if you've been swimmin' with bilge rats," Jackie said as I pulled myself onto shore. I sputtered, choking on both disappointment and salt water. I hadn't caught even one fish for my efforts all day.

"It's just salt water," I reply indignantly, ringing the ocean out of my long tendrils. "You should be used to the smell." I whip my hair around and hope some of the spray lands on his face.

"Aye, but not on a Lassie-Lucy." He winks at me.

"Watch it!" My hand travels reflexively to the pistol holstered at my side. Jackie has no idea the gun has no bullets.

"All right, all right," he chuckles.

After I'm dry I set about creating a dinner, of sorts. By the time it's finished, the sun has set. "Toasted coconut again," I say, grinding my teeth, the desire for fish coating my wanting taste buds. The hot coals snap, as the makeshift spit turns.

Jackie nods and rolls another swig of the contents of his black bottle of rum down his throat. He happily takes his portion. "Thank you, lass," he says. Wiping his mouth, he flips me another coin. *It's the price we've agreed to for every week I cook his meals on this island. I'm starting to amass quite a pile,* I think to myself. Jackie stares at me with those glassy blue eyes, and I feel as if my skin is going to leap off my body.

We chew in silence.

I tilt my head back, listening. The ocean has its own sounds. At night, it seems to sing a song, pulsing through the palms and moving steadily with the rhythm of the waves. I know Jackie hears it too, and that's why he plays. And sings. His voice carries over the waters, seeming to stretch on for miles. This time, the ocean seems to sing back to him.

> *Devil's Doubloon*
> *Show a leg*
> *All you mates*
> *The deeps reg*
> *Open her blackey gates*
> *Tie that dawg*
> *to the yardarm*
> *And smartly*
> *Offer yer charms.*

He sings for hours, and I grow sleepy, enchanted by the call of the ocean and the stories weaved in his music. But I'll not sleep before he nods off first. My fingers are gripped around my pistol the entire night. There is just something about the way he looks at me.

"Lass," he says as my eyes droop.

"Hmmm..?"

"My mates'll be on soon. Enjoy some rum with me before they come." He throws the jug at the sand at my feet.

"Your mates?" My eyes splay open, and I bolt to my feet. This is the first time I have heard Jackie mention anyone else.

"Aye, the song'll bring them, sure ya can bet yer eyes. Like a siren." This sends a wave of shivers through my body. I'd wanted to be rescued, but not by anyone like Jackie.

"Here it comes," Jackie says, his voice whipped with gusto.

A ship draws near the island, black sails and low hull scraping over the water. I gasp as it glides into the sand and I contemplate running, but Jackie offers an assured smile. I don't know anything about the type of hierarchy on a ship like Jackie's, but I know one thing for sure. Jackie is respected and feared by everyone. With his confidence and his bluster, any man would treat him respectfully, thug or not.

"Ye'd be keelhauled if you took any longer, Benito!" Jackie barks, as a barrel-chested man saunters off the boat into the sand, followed by a band of ruffians.

"Sorry Captain, we weren't sure you'd made it," Benito replies, eyes downcast.

"Captain?" My disbelieving voice cries. "You're a captain?"

"Captain Dibolito," Benito says. "Captain, you didn't tell her?"

Jackie bows and flourishes his hands as he says, "Guilty."

I fume and contemplate throwing coconuts. The men from the ship leer at me all the while. "Are you ready to leave this island, or do you want to go on like a bilge-sucking baby longer?" Captain Jackie Dibolito asks.

"I'm ready to leave," I decide, smoothing my dress.

"Captain, did you tell her the price?" One of the members of his crew asks as I near the ship.

Jackie breaks into a wide grin. "Ruining my fun, aren't you, Davey?" The men burst into laughter.

"Fine! To step on my ship means ya leave all yer honor and dignity behind. No one but our kind can set foot on her deck. You must become a member of the Devil's Doubloon crew."

My mind runs blank as I stare at my only chance of leaving the island and an escaping from years of coconuts. I sigh and roll my shoulders. I just couldn't become a member of Jackie's crew.

"I'll stay," the words croak out of my mouth.

"I admire you, I do, lass. But you'll not be getting off the island now. You and your honor'll have to keep one another company. That pile of coins I've left you won't bring a ship."

An Afterword to this story is on page 244.

19

THIEVES OF THE SEAS

by
Mirta Oliva

1596

Baron Lockhart Lyonstaff of Southshire was leaving London with his new secretary, Marianne. They were special guests aboard a big ship headed for the Caribbean where the Baron planned to finish his book, *My Encounter with the Thieves of the Seas*. It was only fitting that he would choose Port Royal in Jamaica to learn more about those criminals who would trick sailors in order to seize their ships. Those robbers knew that the vessels were transporting precious cargo of gold and silver from the New World to the Old.

Five days later, before dinner at the Merry Weather, the two guests went outside for a while. The writing was progressing enough that they could often spend casual time together. With each unofficial encounter, Marianne's infatuation for the handsome Lord Lockhart of Southshire grew stronger. How could she suppress her feelings in front of this gentle person…?

After some more uneventful days at sea, the Captain announced that they would be arriving at Port Royal in a couple of days – only if the fast-approaching storm would go away. Lord Lyonstaff and his secretary were entering the deck to check on the weather when they felt the big waves furiously embracing the vessel. Soon they heard a commotion and – to their bewilderment – the crew was already letting up the sails and carrying out other emergency measures. Rain began to pour, and they both hurried back to their rooms. Holding Marianne's hands affectionately, the Baron asked her to get her most important possessions and to rush to his cabin. After gathering some belongings, the blushing girl knocked on the gentleman's door ... this was all that Marianne could remember of what would have been a wonderful evening - other than recalling the sounds of some instruments playing Medieval chamber music – presaging that old shipwreck's curse.

"Marianne, please open your eyes..." Lord Lyonstaff repeated over and over, tenderly running his fingers through the young woman's hair. Finally, he could see Marianne's hazel eyes looking softly at him with great admiration.

"Our ship capsized, and we ended up on this island. I guess I had held you so close that we ended up tightly embraced on that large piece of timber that brought us here. However, I haven't seen any other survivors ashore," the Baron blurted out.

"Oh, Lord, what are we going to do now?" Marianne lamented.

"You must not worry. I will take care of you until you are safe back home," Lord Lyonstaff solemnly declared. "Let's see if I can find us some shelter."

As the Baron walked away, he saw two trunks being pushed by the waves over the sand. Soon he was able to haul them back behind the bushes. He had read enough about the thieves of the seas to know that they may have to give away some treasures in order to survive from violent encounters. As he carefully opened the smaller trunk, he was happy to find linen and toiletries. The bigger one contained many numbered small locked boxes full of gold coins belonging to the ship's passengers. Soon he had buried them in different areas in order to give only one to each attacking vessel displaying a skeleton flag. A while later, Lord Lyonstaff observed a huge crate coming ashore, abruptly stopping on the dry sand. He used rocks as a hammer to open the crate. It took him a while but what a surprise! It was full of preserved foodstuff and bottles of wine. The food should last them at least a week.

Before it got dark, the Baron started looking for shelter. He emptied the crate and hauled it toward a tree, covering the bottom with leaves and a blanket from the trunk. Now Marianne could feel somewhat protected there. He would sleep by her side. Around midnight a young man was loudly demanding pieces of gold. Aha! They were being robbed! Trying not to wake up Marianne, the Baron pulled a box with gold coins and a bottle of wine that he had purposely hidden in the sand next to him and handed it to the boy. "That's all I have of value, you can have it. The girl is ill, please leave in peace." The boy believed that was all they possessed and gladly left for his ship, not before surprising them with a cooking pot.

Two days later, detecting a distant vessel, the Baron asked Marianne to hide, pulled out a box full of coins and hid it in the sand along with the remaining bottles of wine.

The arriving violent visitors were quickly appeased with the bounty that was being handed to them. The moment was ripe for Lord Lyonstaff to plead with the more dominant thief to take him to Port Royal in Jamaica – his original destination – one of several safe havens for the greatest scums on earth. Since he had made Marianne aware of his plan – possibly the only way to return to England alive – the worried Baron left without saying good-bye.

On the way to Jamaica, a young thief began harassing the Baron, asking him for more coins. One minute he pretended to be nice and the next he would pull out a knife threatening the gentleman - all until a ranking thief threw the vicious boy overboard.

After dropping the Baron at the port, the crew of thieves quickly left with their treasures – enough to last them until their next "stop."

A port captain accepted to rescue Marianne in exchange for gold. He would then take them back to London where the Baron could rewrite his book – now with a bigger story to tell. It did not take long for Marianne to go on board, handing the captain three boxes full of gold coins. Lord Lyonstaff rushed to embrace Marianne, giving her a long kiss on each cheek. That was the beginning of what would be a forever-lasting relationship as husband and wife.

An Afterword to this story is on page 245.

20

A CAT'S TALE

by
Elaine Faber

A metal bucket crashed inches from Esme's head. She snatched a small fish from the display case and ran. "Scram! Witch from Hell! Begone, I say, and don't come back!" Out of sight from the shopkeeper in a nearby alley, she devoured her ill-gotten gains.

Her pink tongue licked one sticky foot, swept it across her ears and down the side of her black face, repeating the process until every trace of fish smell was gone, and her ebony body glistened in the sunlight. Having completed her toilette, she lay down to observe the harbor activities and chose a ship for her next voyage.

Admired and much sought after by the harbor captains for her skills as a *ratter,* she must be alert, lest she be shanghaied onto a buccaneer's ship infested with rats. Without a capable working cat aboard, rats could overrun a ship with resulting deadly disease. Esme had no desire to spend months on such a ship.

Esme's attention was diverted as she scratched an itch on the small of her back. Suddenly, the world went dark. The reek of sour oats filled her nostrils. She was flipped upside down in a filthy sack.

"Gottcha, you little she-devil! Cappin' will be mighty pleased. I bring him the best ratter in town!"

Esme was flung into a dark hold. No sooner had her eyes adjusted to the dark, the unmistakable odor of *rat* wafted by her delicate nose. She calculated its location, leaped, grabbed the rat, and sunk her teeth through its spine. The thing lay dead. Disgusting!

Esme lay in darkness throughout the night, hungry and thirsty. Then the door of the hold screeched open. Esme hunkered in the shadow of a box as the outline of a head appeared against the morning sky "Hey, cat, air' ye' hungry? Cappin' says I otter' feed ye."

Esme leaped toward freedom. Her toes caught the lip of the deck, and she hung suspended. She pulled herself upward scrabbling to get a purchase with her back feet.

The sailor slammed the lid, catching the end of Esme's tail. She shrieked as the deckle sliced clean through her tail. Leaving a trail of blood, she sprinted down the gangplank. Trembling with pain and dizzy from blood loss, she sought refuge behind a pile of wood.

"What's this? Air' ye' ailin,' cat? Let me help."

Esme lifted her head, responding to the kind voice. The sailor gathered her up and carried her aboard his ship, washed her wound, and fed her spoonfuls of rum and egg. "Ye'll be missin' part a' yer' tail, but I doubt it be keepin' ye' from yer' duties." He stroked Esme's head. "Folks say you be a champion ratter. We be blessed yer' aboard."

With little else to entertain the boisterous crew, they jealously vied for Esme's attention when she favored one above the other.

With luck, there weren't many rats on board this ship; just enough to keep her busy on a boring afternoon. With the besotted crew, good food and the fine weather, life was good.

For sport and riches, the buccaneers attacked frigates loaded with tea, linens, jewelry, and chests of gold coins as they navigated the Caribbean islands.

On a particular day in May of 1789, the jubilant band, having captured a merchant ship the day before, celebrated late into the night, leaving a minimal watch crew. The skull and crossbones hanging from the mast hung limp in the heavy fog.

Unseen by sleepy watchmen, the King's ship stole closer... until volleys of cannons crashed into the unwary pirate ship. The acrid smell of gun power filled the air. Deckhands beat at the flames raging across the deck toward the battered stairs.

Esme slunk behind a barrel, trembling, her heart throbbing.

"All hands, abandon ship! Give me the cat. With her good luck, we may survive." The crew dove toward the waiting lifeboat.

Esme was flung overboard. Hurtling and twisting, fighting the empty air beneath her body, she was caught by eager hands and stuffed beneath the lifeboat seat. The scent of damp rope and sweat assailed Esme's nose.

Whoosh! The topsail exploded in flames. Pieces of burning canvas fluttered up like flaming kites, skittered through the air, and then drifted down, sizzling as they struck the water. Smoke and flames cast a gray and orange glow in the churning water, littered with debris. The flaming mast disappeared beneath the waves. Only a streak of oil and bubbles remained where once a brigand ship had sailed.

Thick fog sheltered the lifeboat from the King's retribution. "Quiet, boys, and row like hell. Iffen' they catch us, we'll hang from the yardarm before nightfall." The castaways rowed until sweat poured from their bodies.

Safe beneath the First Mate's seat, the rhythm of the oars thumping the water lulled Esme into slumber. Though she slept, her tail swayed, as though driven by a different master. For three days the wretched men rowed, thirsty and exhausted until they were picked up by a friendly ship.

In the years that followed, in that distant land, where ships filled the harbor with tall colored sails and men of debatable reputation wagered bags of gold and lifted pots of rum to recount events of that fateful night, they credited the black cat's luck for saving the twelve castaways. The legend of the cat with a stubby tail spread far and wide.

Each spring while preparing to sail, the captains would try to lure Esme onto their ships by inducement or guile, covetous of her skills and good luck. She was ever watchful, refusing to be caught, lest she be taken to a ship not of her choosing. At the last moment before setting sail, she would board the ship of her choice. Legitimate or brigand mattered not. It must be a ship with kind seafarers and plentiful food. A ship not overrun with rats; just enough to test her skills on a long hot, boring afternoon.

An Afterword to this story is on page 246.

21

LAUGHING FATES

by
Laura Stafford

The sound of singing and crashing waves woke Jodee from a dense sleep. He opened his eyes to stars and a crescent moon against endless black. He knew those stars like his own hand, but tonight they seemed foreign and distant.

The singing stopped. "I wondered if you were ever going to join the living again." Jodee knew that voice—a woman, raspy but with a lilt that sounded like a bird.

He sat up. Alonia was poking at a small fire where fish roasted on a rock. She gave him a devil's stare. "Funny," she said, "that it should be the most powerful and the lowliest to survive, eh?"

Jodee rubbed the sand from his face. The lowliest? Yes, he was just the deckhand, but Jodee had certainly done his fair share of raping and pillaging, and perhaps he was destined for better (or worse) things.

"Aye," Alonia continued. "But there are worse things than being lost here, aren't there?"

Alonia always talked in riddles. He hated that. The captain seemed to understand her, his seer, his gypsy woman, his advisor and mistress.

He looked about their surroundings and saw the stretching strip of sand, pummelled by waves, and palm trees behind. The beach was littered with debris and dead bodies.

"It's just me an' you?" he wondered.

"Everyone else dead. Yous was the only one breathing. And dis one..." Alonia pointed down the beach. In the moonlit distance Jodee could see a figure jumping in and out of the waves.

"Who is that?"

"No sayin'. He has been here a long time, I figures. He doesn't know his name. Says the sirens called in his ship to steal his rum and gold, but I found both in a cave up there." Now she pointed the opposite direction.

Gold? Jodee said nothing. "How long have we been here?"

"Two sun rises, far as I can tell."

Gold... Jodee thought again, pondering how much.

Alonia knelt in front of him, handing him a jug of rum and fish on a large, unidentifiable leaf. "I knows what ye be thinkin', lad."

Of course she knew, Jodee thought, she was a witch. And she would want to keep the gold for herself. Why wouldn't she?

Jodee threw the leaf and fish bones into the fire, stood and stretched, absently shaking the sand from his boots. Alonia eyed him intently as he strode away and down the beach.

The man was dressed in rags, caterwauling in the surf, screeching and laughing at the waves. Jodee wondered how long this man had been here, knowing by the length of his matted beard and hair that it had been an extended duration. He was holding a large cast iron pot, throwing it down when the sea came in and lifting it up over his head when the tide went out.

If he hadn't been making lunatic animal noises, Jodee would have thought he was dancing.

Boldly, Jodee walked straight up to the man. He opened his arms to Jodee, still laughing. "It be You!" he exclaimed. "You free me!"

Jodee snatched the heavy black pot from his weak grasp, swung it in a tight arc and walloped the man on the side of his head. He went down smiling. The crazy had left his eyes that began to fade to a dull grey. Jodee hit him in the head till there was nothing left of the man's face.

"Ayuh," Jodee said to the blood in the foamy surf, "It be me who freed ya."

He carried the pot back to the fire where Alonia sat with her back to him. Approaching soft and quietly, Jodee was surprised into stillness when she spoke.

"I'll be laughing with the Fates when they punish you," Alonia's voice was a whisper, but it echoed over the ocean like a thousand birds rising from the trees. "I pray you live a thousand years with your greed."

Jodee smashed the cast iron against her skull.

* * *

There was more gold than could be counted. There were more days than could be counted. He grabbed his chin and realized his beard was as long and matted as the crazy, nameless man.

But the gold was no friend. And at night, when the moon was full, Jodee would scream and cry to the waves like a siren calling in the ships.

An Afterword to this story is on page 247.

22

SALVATION

by
Neil Carroll Ellison

We'd been adrift for nearly fourteen days. I knew the passage of time by the moon's cycle. The night of our sinking had been dark; half of a waxing moon lit the debris that had been our ship. Tonight we had a full moon by which to see.

Straining my eyes against the darkness, I spied a shadow on the horizon and called out to Markeson. "Do you see it too? There. It dances in my sight, bedeviling me. I do not know if it's real."

Markeson confirmed my sighting.

We broke out the oars from beneath the gunwale and turned the lifeboat toward the land of our salvation. Our target was defined only by a deeper blackness in the sky. Its presence blocked the stars from the heavens. We heaved our backs into our strokes, pulling hard as we headed toward that hole in the night.

The frantic rhythm of our rowing began to wear on our hands. The rough wood tore at our calloused flesh each time the paddles struck the water; our arms began to tire of their seemingly endless fight against the resistance of the sea.

Markeson knew that our current efforts would not save us. He was a skilled sailor and realized the futility of fighting the ocean, "Slow down. Listen to the sea. Do you hear her singing? Row to her song, honor her with the dance of our oars."

Listening to the music, we rowed effortlessly, as if entranced.

Our boat struck the beach just as the sun kissed our faces to awaken us. We had rowed through the night. Climbing from the boat, I fell to the sand and embraced it like a lost lover. We stumbled toward the palms in search of shade and sustenance.

Food was plentiful. We were blessed with mangoes, coconuts, and plantains.

A few days after our arrival, we were greeted by another lost soul. He said his name was Peavey. He told us that he had been cast away by a privateer as punishment for secreting food to an ill shipmate. "My crime was not severe enough to warrant immediate death, but the captain had to make an example of me. He sent me off in a raft, and I found myself here as though I was called to this cay."

He showed us how to build shelter for protection and how to spear fish in the shallow water. I was thankful that he was generous with his knowledge. I wondered about the source of his bountiful rum, but said nothing.

One morning, we awoke to see a ship sailing toward our island. Markeson and I took to high ground to watch its arrival. Peavey was noticeably absent.

She dropped anchor in the deep waters and lowered her small boats. Sailors wearing tattered cloth came ashore. We saw Peavey greet them. It wasn't long before they began to search the island for us.

There was nowhere to hide. The buccaneers discovered us hiding under a pile of fallen palms. They marched us to their boat and took us to their ship. Peavey rode along quietly.

If our previous home had been heaven, this was surely hell. The ship was black with tar to aid in waterproofing the wooden hull. The crew stank of unwashed humanity. We were held on deck while the leader of the shore team left to alert the captain.

The crew looked away as their leader emerged from below deck. His uniform was as tattered as those of his crew, but I could still make out the insignia of the British Royal Navy. He had been an officer, now he was a rogue.

"Peavey! Wha' 'ave ye brough' me? Were ye sharin' tales of my treasure?"

Peavey looked nervous. He was wringing his hands. Averting his eyes from the captain, he said, "They are just two lost sailors, sir. They arrived only days ago."

Markeson stepped forward, "We sail for no man or country anymore. It's been a month since our ship sank. Your friend helped us survive on this island. I demand that you release us back to shore. We are of no consequence to you."

The captain raised an eyebrow and smiled a crooked, black-toothed grin. "Aye, lad. Ye may na' be of my crew, but I canna' have ye speakin' ta me like tha' on my ship."

He turned to his crew. "Keelhaul this insolent bastard!"

There was no hope for Markeson now. He was tied at hand and foot. Secured to long ropes that were handled by the crew, he was thrown over the bow to be drug along the bottom of the ship.

Instead of running him across the ship's beam, his punishment was to be pulled along the full length of the hull. Thousands of razor sharp barnacles and massive wooden splinters awaited his passage. He couldn't scream out in pain as it would ensure immediate death by drowning.

We began to see small blooms of crimson blood blossom in the clear Caribbean water. The crew was walking him too slowly, he could not survive this torture. They hauled his body up from the stern and displayed him on deck.

Markeson's body was ravaged by the keelhauling. Skin was flayed from his back. His head and arms dangled by sinew. The captain kicked Markeson's lifeless body then looked at me.

"Ye'll be joinin' us, won't ye lad." It wasn't a question.

* * *

When I was a child, I saw the notations at the far edges of a sailing map that read, *Here There Be Monsters*. I had no idea what they really meant. Characterized by fanciful sea creatures, these fictions hid a darker truth that escaped my young mind.

The monsters of which they whispered were men who had forsaken their humanity for the pleasure of plunder—

men once devout, but now demonic—men who had lost all hope in mankind and discovered their salvation in hell.

Heaven help me.

An Afterword to this story is on page 248.

23

WITCH'S ISLAND

by
Glenda Reynolds

Captain Jon Devon stood at the wheel as he sailed his ship, *The Devil's Plunder*, towards his home island of Jamaica. He pillaged the Caribbean as he sailed a fast caravel ship under a black flag with cross bones. Devon was a huge imposing figure dressed in dark weathered clothing. His hair resembled that of a lion's mane with his dreadlocks framing his perfect, unearthly face. The wind ruffled his black hat, but it always managed to stay on his head with the front brim turned up. A double holster was strapped across his chest with two pistols in it. He wore a silver talisman given to him by his maker, Zafrina, which allowed him to be a "day walker". Although he was a pleasure-seeking, dung-souled ruffian in his past life, he was ten times more now that he was an immortal. Only one thing reined him in—his love for a beautiful Jamaican woman named Desiree who sailed with him at all times.

The sea became increasingly stormy as his ship approached an uncharted island. The sound of long horns and drums was carried on the wind. Even though he tried as hard as he possibly could, Captain Devon could not navigate the ship away from the mysterious island. A very old, dilapidated lighthouse stood on the craggy rocks like a beacon of doom. To his horror and that of his crew, the ship plunged headlong into the shoreline of huge imposing boulders, which stood like black fingers waiting to grasp the unsuspecting vessel. With one giant wave of the sea, the ship became wedged between the boulders. The force of the wave and the quick stoppage of the ship caught in the boulders sent Devon and his shipmate Jamal overboard. The two of them managed to crawl ashore despite the pounding waves.

They immediately noticed many weathered trees on the shoreline that looked to be sculpted by the wind and sea until they stood bare, smooth, and bent over. Suddenly a man's face came to life on the tree trunk.

"Ye beware o' the witch of this island. Leave now while ye can lest ye become part of the island."

"How long ha' ya bin here, man?" asked Devon.

"Thirty years now. We are all doomed, cursed by Raven. Ye be warned." The face on the tree became silent. Devon and Jamal noticed other men who had been trapped inside of trees on the shoreline.

Devon found a club that he found floating in the surf; he offered it to Jamal for protection. Together they strode into the interior of the island. Surely there was treasure to be found on here. They crossed a small glade at the foot of two mountains. A cave was spotted at the base. They made a torch out of old leg bones that lit the way down to the belly of the island.

They came upon a female who was working on her spells. Her pet snake was wrapped around her shoulders. The clothing she wore hinted of African-Caribbean origin. She knew the black magic of voodoo as well as being a "gifted" immortal. The room was filled with jugs of rum and loose and bagged gold coin, possibly stolen from her many victims that were lead to her island by way of the magical island music.

"My name is Raven. What do you seek on my island?"

"Dat gold fo' starters, girl," replied Devon.

"There is a price to pay for dis gold, Mista."

"I'm Captain Jon Devon. What price would you be meanin'?

"You would make a fine addition to my island." She came close to him and ran her hand up his arm. "For you, I would make my mate," she said with seductive eyes.

Devon would never betray his love for Desiree. "Woman, all the gold in the Caribbean would not be enough for that." He turned to go back to his ship.

Raven was not used to refusals. She watched his retreating figure and that of Jamal's in disbelief. When the two men arrived back at the shore, their shipmates had just pulled the ship free of the boulders with the mooring ropes. Devon turned to see that Raven had followed them there. Desiree was watching the two from the bow.

"Don't be stupid, Devon," Raven derided him. "She will grow old an' die one day whereas we could spend eternity together on de high seas. She is nothing but a puny human, food for de immortals."

"Don't vex me so. Go 'way, witch."

"Don't be a fool. Your decision affects both you and your mate."

"Nothing you can do will eva change me mind."

"So be it."

Raven raised her hand and at once the silver talisman that Devon wore flew from his neck and landed in her palm.

"Wha' gwan? I need dat to survive a sea! De sun will turn me to ash without it."

"You will do well without it, and you will do well without something else too."

Raven looked at his ship where Desiree was watching from the bow. Raven extended her hand toward the mortal as she recited the dark curse that would bind them both. Desiree's skin became as weathered wood as she climbed over the bow of the ship, extended her arms on either side of her, and hung there as the ship's figurehead. In this state she was dead to Jon Devon, neither speaking nor moving. Her eyes stared out into nothing.

Devon whirled around to confront Raven who had disappeared from sight. Upon seeing his beloved for the first time in her cursed state, a mournful cry was wrenched from his lips and broke the silence of the night. From that night forward Jon Devon was cursed to remain in his coffin by day; Desiree was cursed to be the ship's figurehead by night. They were forever together yet eternally apart. Devon appropriately renamed his ship *The Cursed Leviathan* as he continued to wreak havoc on the Caribbean Sea.

An Afterword to this story is on page 249.

24

THE TENTH GOLD PIECE

by
Timothy Paul

Scott's heart raced as he stood at the edge of a watery abyss. A dark dream of death gave way to water lapping lazily around his heels.

He woke to a bright sun burning his skin in places that should be covered. Elbows dug into wet sand as he pushed himself to sit up. His Levis and Green Bay Packers T-Shirt were hung to dry in the crook of a flame tree. His sandals and briefs baked on a large rock beside it.

To his left, the foul-mouthed extradition officer was wrapped around the trunk of a fig tree. Steel cuffs held his arms together. Red-eyed and cussing a blue streak, the lawman now sported a ridiculously wide-brimmed hat.

Scott's wrists were now free. *But how? What happened?* A sudden churning of water on a windless day had tossed the chartered yacht by the strength of a gale. He remembered the captain twisting the dials on the radio. "Mayday! Mayday!" No response. The airwaves were empty. No, not empty. Old radio shows. And then someone whistled an oddly familiar melody that rose and fell in a minor key.

"So you're finally awake, mate," said a soft voice behind him.

Twisting around, he looked up into the royal blue eyes of a tall slender woman. Long braids interwoven with a bright red bandana held her raven black hair behind her shoulders. Fitted with a soft white blouse and khaki pants, she looked as if she walked off the set of an Errol Flynn movie.

Unconsciously Scott pulled his legs toward his chest to cover his embarrassment. "I take it you're my angel?"

"Are you asking if I was the one that cut the shackles from that foul tempered gent over yonder? That would be me. I also freed you from that fancy outfit."

Thoughts of modesty vanished as this temptress from another time was suddenly the only thing on his mind. A mischievous smirk crossed her face accompanied by a flirtatious wink.

"Would you like something to eat?" she asked. A bowl of tropical fruits suddenly appeared in her hands. Kneeling to the ground, she set the bowl down before him.

"Who are you?" Scott tried to continue, but his question trailed off as her small gilded wrist rose to her chest. His eyes transfixed onto matching golden buttons holding her blouse in place. Fleeting memories of the 21st century lost their grip as a stone goblet materialized in his hand. Cheap rum filled his belly, igniting a dangerous rebellion unrivaled by his reckless past. Filled with rum, consciousness returned, yet he felt no effects from the drink.

"Anne Bonny," said the woman, once again standing at his side as if she had been waiting for him and none of her devious schemes had taken place.

"What?"

"You asked who I am."

"What do you want?"

"No more than you've given. Your vessel was a strange one, and she won't sail in our seas. Not worth troubling Davey Jones about. So you see, you're of no help for taking us off this island. But that's all well and good. I've got my own way off. Of course, it will require sharing the booty with me crew."

"Booty?"

"The money you spoke of in your enchantment. The currency your captor so coldly removed from your possession."

"You bewitched me to learn my secrets?"

The woman's smile vanished and was replaced with urgency. "You must now retrieve it, or we'll both be one with the wind. Once you have it, meet me on the western shore."

Scott watched her set off in the direction of the sinking sun.

With the lawman secured, Scott looked to the flame tree. Baggy breeches and a leather vest had replaced his jeans and t-shirt. Not exactly his style, but it was better than the officer's cheap suit.

He turned his attention to what looked like a scallywag on a tree, wearing a wide hat that covered a slumping head and shoulders. "Hey, warden," he shouted sarcastically.

The man on the tree didn't flinch. Scott took the hat from the drooping head and jumped back. Staring through him were the hollow sockets and death grin of a skeleton. The oddly familiar melody echoed through the jaws of the dead man.

A life of smuggling had taught Scott to embrace his fear and use it to advantage. In that moment he knew he'd never see home again. Was this the sentence for his many crimes? Energized by the unknown, he searched the agent's pockets for drug money that he had taken as evidence. There was bounty enough to buy passage on any vessel. Suspecting she'd demand it all, he tucked a small wad under an armband, which he hadn't noticed until now.

Anne Bonny was silhouetted on the shore. She signaled to a rowboat, which was making its way inland. Anchored beyond was a great wooden sailing ship. A bold black flag waved atop the center mast bearing a white skull floating over crossed swords. Anne Bonny turned to face him with a flintlock pistol in hand. "I'll need the coins you fetched from the lawman."

"They're not exactly coins," Scott replied.

"I'll take them just the same."

Reluctantly he reached into his deep baggy pocket and wrapped his fingers around a stack of large round coins. He pulled out all but one and opened a shaky hand.

"Looks to be about eight gold pieces from where I stand," Anne said.

He took a quick count. "You have good eyes."

"I know gold. Eight pieces will divide just well enough to satisfy my crew. That last one in your pocket will buy your life."

A sense of strange powers at hand brought hesitation. "And if I find one more, will that buy me a place aboard your boat?"

A wry smile slowly grew across Anne Bonny's face. "You impress me, Jack."

"My name's Scott," he said, and handed her ten gold coins.

She produced a leather belt wrapped around an ebony-handled dagger and tossed it to him. "'Tis nae' more. My crew'll know ye as Calico Jack."

An Afterword to this story is on page 250.

25

FINDERS KEEPERS

by
Douglas G. Clarke

Another wave washed over her, pushing her farther up the beach. Margaret looked more like a drowned rat than a high lady. The folds of her dress wrapped around her legs, binding them. The red of her corset was like blood peeking out from beneath her white blouse.

John ran down the beach. He hesitated as he approached, looking up and down the shoreline. He stared out to sea, watching the waves break against the reef, listening to the same whistling tones that he had heard when he had been shipwrecked here. His eyes returned to the woman in the surf. He reached down and scooped her up into his arms.

Margaret woke beside a warm fire, a blanket covering her. She looked around and saw her dress and blouse draped across a bush on the other side of the fire. She shivered.

"Ye be awake? Jolly good," John said as he entered the firelight.

"Ye undressed me!"

"I could not let ye die 'o cold after ye made it ashore." John threw some of the sticks he was carrying onto the fire.

"Did ye heartily enjoy it?"

"Me Lady. Ye pierce me soul." John dropped the sticks and placed his hands against his chest. "To be honest... it wasn't completely unenjoyable... much like carryin' ye water-soaked self here."

Margaret looked away from John, staring into the fire while John sat next to her. "Some rum may warm ye," he said while holding out a flask to her.

Margaret grabbed the flask from him. "Scoundrel. 'Tis was me salty sea-dog 'o a father's. I should have ye keel hauled."

"Ye'll be wanting ye dagger back then?"

If it wasn't for the damp mat of hair that framed Margaret's face, the look of her eyes could have killed.

John tossed the dagger into the sand by her. "I just didn't want ye to roll over and hurt yourself, or wake up before we met and kill me in me sleep."

"What makes ye think I won't now?"

"Me eternal optimism... 'n ye'll be famished in th' mornin'. By th' way, mind if I have a wee bit 'o that rum? I did get a wee bit chilled carryin' ye here."

Margaret hefted the flask, took a long drink from it, and then tossed it to John.

"Makes us even."

"Expensive rum."

John leaned back and closed his eyes. Margaret pushed the dagger into its scabbard and fell into a restless sleep.

The smell of eggs greeted Margaret as she awoke. "It's not much," John said, "but I do what I can. Seagull eggs and toasted coconut." Despite herself, Margaret's stomach growled.

"Be off ahead 'n get dressed, I won't look."

"That be just because ye be a smart jim laddie. Ye be knowin' I'd kill ye if ye did."

John laughed.

Margaret got up, her red corset and panties contrasting with the lush green of the jungle, her pale skin catching the yellows of the fire. "Ye can look now."

John turned towards her and placed the iron pan of food in front of her. "How long have ye been stranded here?"

John paused before answering. "It be hard to shout, th' weeks all seem to blend into each other. A pair, maybe three years."

"Alone all that time?"

"Thar have been others washed up on shore, but ye be the first to make it through th' night – ye missed th' reef."

"I may have judged you wrongly. To survive on ye own fer so long, 'n ye cook. What other surprises do ye hold?"

"I have explored 'tis entire God forsaken island more times that you can imagine, but I have been rewarded. Others have come to 'tis island, not as ye and I, but in longboats. They came to bury their treasures 'n I watched. When they left I took a share. Ye want to spy wit' ye eye?"

A beautiful smile formed on Margaret's face, "I'd love to."

John retrieved a chest and proudly showed Margaret its gold and silver.

Hearing something, Margaret stood and looked through the trees towards the beach beyond. "Quick John, a ship has come fer us."

Margaret grabbed one of the chest's handles and pulled John behind her.

Reaching the beach they stopped - these were not the king's men.

"Hoi Captain, where have ye been? I see you have some treasure."

"Aye, but 'tis all mine." With that Margaret kissed John and gave him a swat. "And his gold and silver, too."

An Afterword to this story is on page 251.

26

THE TECHNICIAN

by
Clement Chow

When the Somali technician regained consciousness, he saw the insignia of three chevrons and two rockers on the left shoulder of his rescuer. A gunnery sergeant from the Marine Corps, he could still tell after his close death encounter. Even though he was just a mere technician of the *Ocean Saviors* affiliation, he could memorize all the ranks, insignias, and pay grades of major armed forces around the world. It was a personal hobby of his. "Why you save me?" he managed to ask after coughing out most of the water from his lungs.

The marine shrugged. "You're welcome," he held him up to sit against a boulder. "The name's Drake Marshal by the way."

The technician blinked. "You know we make yours and ours ships ruined because of fight." The shipwrecks of USS Ramage and three hijacked Thai trawlers lay nearby. "Why you help me? You know I am one of them."

"All I know is that we're stranded on this island for the time being. Enough people have died, and I don't want to see another death today. Not on my watch."

The technician stared into Drake's resolute eyes, then wiped his right hand on his pants. "My name is Erasto Abdi Asad."

Drake scratched his head, confused with the new language. "I'll call you Eraser for now," he looked around the deserted beach. "Looks like you and I are the only survivors. What now?" He pointed at the stranded USS Ramage. "All the communications, GPS, and navigations are down. There's nothing else to do from my end."

"That a problem," Erasto patted his own back, nervous as to why the marine didn't arrest him. Then he felt it, a certain 10 grams of weight lost from his neck. He reached his right hand for his chest, stopped breathing, and continued clutching his chest until it turned a faint red. "My pendant, my wife pendant is missing!"

Drake looked up at the burning Thai trawler. "You mean it's on your ship?" Three more explosions erupted for the three seconds they laid sight on it. "Too dangerous, Eraser. There's fire everywhere. Better to save your life than your locket. You'll see her anyways when you get back."

"No, I cannot." The technician looked at the ground, eyes focused on the sand between his fingers. "One year ago, she passed." Tears formed in each of the technician's four crevices.

"Sorry to hear that." Drake looked at the rustling palm trees. "I got a wife back home who's been really supportive, but she still cries every time when I go out on another tour. It ain't easy, doing what's right, having your loved ones support you, and to fight the feeling of wishing to think the same logical way they do." The logical person wouldn't make a living by risking death. His head pointed towards the trawler. "Let's move out."

"I cannot. You cannot come. I very thankful you save me. I cannot ask anymore."

"Ah, you can treat me 10 lobsters later. Now let's go, before I change my mind."

* * *

Shrapnel, whether encased in flames or not, flew in multiple directions. Some of them burned holes into Drake's and Erasto's uniforms, yet they didn't let out the faintest squeal. With the trawler lying on its starboard side, the pair ran along the port-side windows. Minor explosions ruptured back and forth as they ran towards the bridge.

Erasto raised his right arm as he first entered the control room. Drake followed shortly, but it was only after when he realized both of Erasto's arms were up, with another ocean robber pointing an AKM at them.

"It okay, Captain Asad. He my friend. His name is Drake Marshal."

The captain aimed closer at the intruder with widened eyes. "Air Marshall? I kill you right now!" Before he could aim at Drake's head, an explosion behind him caused a flying bolt and washer to pierce his. With his last remaining consciousness, he pulled the trigger and shot three rounds, two of which scraped the marine's shoulder while the third went through it.

Drake held in his scream as he fell to the ground and rested against a shattered drawer. "Get what you came here for," he muttered to Erasto.

The technician slid down to the right side to his former GPS station, smothered the flames, and retrieved his locket.

Though he had a difficult time holding up Drake's massive body from his uninjured left side, the pair had a rather uneventful trip off the ship and onto the shore's white beach sands.

But before the marine's wound could be treated, a voice emerged from behind the hijacked ship. "This is good surprise," a monkey-like voice said.

Two muscular men walked into view, 15 feet from the injured marine. The man on the right sported a wrench, while the other had a rocket-propelled grenade.

Erasto instantly recognized his two fellow robbers from before the shipwreck. "Asad!" he called out to the one on the right. "We need to help him. He save my life."

"Shat up, GPS man!" Asad replied. "No food on this island! But he make good meat."

The two ex-militiamen formed the muscle of the ocean robber trade. They cracked their knuckles as they approached with salamander smiles.

"I won't blame you if you join back with them," Drake muttered.

Erasto stood up and gazed at his former comrades. They only looked at the marine who lay on the floor, paying no attention to him.

"As far as they know, you're still on their side," the marine continued to whisper.

Erasto turned on his heels to face Drake and reached for his TT-30 in his right pocket.

"That's right. It's the only way for you to survive and to get what you want. I would've done the same."

The ex-technician shook his head. "I see too many innocent deaths. I not gonna let that happen again. Not on my watch."

An Afterword to this story is on page 252.

27

MAROONED!

by
Connie Flanagan

My husband Darrel, knowing I was a homebody, had nonetheless planned a Caribbean cruise for our second honeymoon. One evening while stargazing, we heard ethereal music coming from the sky. Many of the other passengers, even deaf old Jacob who was celebrating his 50th anniversary with his wife Carol, soon heard it as well. The deck became crowded with our fellow travellers, all craning their necks to locate the heavenly host.

Suddenly the boat scraped bottom deafeningly. I didn't recall much until I awoke with my face planted on a beach. I was alive! The lack of human sounds, however, was foreboding. Checking myself for any serious injuries, I sat up and looked about. The beach was narrow, verging onto jungle. About 20 metres away, I spotted what looked like coloured rags. As I drew closer, I recognised Jacob. I approached from the direction in which he was facing, so as not to startle him. He looked up at me with a pathetic visage and motioned for me to come closer.

"Is it just us?" he whispered.

"I think so," I replied, glancing once more about the narrow beach.

"Thank God! I couldn't take that woman for another day!" he exclaimed. As he began to chuckle mirthfully, I realised he meant his wife Carol. I started to laugh, too, until we were both laughing so hard we were holding our stomachs. "I've pretended to be deaf for the last ten years," he sputtered, "just so I wouldn't have to talk to her!"

"So you really did hear the music?" I finally managed, wiping tears from my eyes.

"Yep. I think it was a Siren," he replied seriously.

We both whirled around as a voice replied, "Nope. That'd of been me. Nathan."

A rugged looking young man, without a whisker to his chin, stood before us. His eyes were dark and filled with mirth. A navy kerchief covered his brown hair, and he wore a blousy shirt that would not look out of place in 17th century France. His breeches were held up with a piece of rope rather than a belt.

"It's been my sorry lot ta work with a crew o' bandits by luring ships toward the reef out there so's they can rob 'em," he explained with a wave of his arm toward the ocean.

Just as I was about to indignantly lash out at him, he went on to explain that his "mates" would be returning that night to check for survivors who could perhaps be held for ransom. Jacob and I looked apprehensively at one another. With our spouses dead, who would pay money for us? I could see myself becoming a wench on a ship flying the Jolly Roger, while Jacob would be fed to the fish. Alarmed, I turned to our informer. "What can we do?!" I demanded.

"Well," he sighed, "T'aint much ye can do, I'm afeared. They've had me heah on this island for two yeahs now. When they found out I could draw ships by singin', they decided not ta sell me, but ta keep me as a crew member."

"How did you make that music?" Jacob inquired.

Our captor shrugged and drew a deep breath before opening his throat and warbling at the heavens.

"Goodness!" Jacob exclaimed. "That's like nothing I've ever heard! It sounds like the entire choir of heaven!"

Nathan shrugged and replied, "I'm not from aroun' heah. My ship crashed some time back as we was headin' for home."

"And where would that be?" I asked suspiciously. I was beginning to notice some oddities about him—his hair was moving like lively tentacles, his nose was flattened to appear as almost just two holes in his face, and his throat was unusually thick.

"That'd be one o' the galaxies next to your 'un," he answered. Looking into his eyes, which I suddenly realised were black without pupils, I drew back in disgust and fear. Jacob, on the other hand, looked as pleased as he had when he learned that Carol was gone. He whistled low.

"Now that is some tale. Do you have any other abilities that might help all of us, yourself included, out of this situation in which we find ourselves?"

Nathan offered to lead us to his camp. We could each take one item from his arsenal if we thought it would help.

At the camp there was a plethora of oddities. It was impossible to know what everything was at a glance. Just as

Jacob and I were scrutinising the objects, our host raised his head and whispered, "They a' comin' fo' ya."

"I didn't hear anything," argued "deaf" Jacob.

"No, I smells the rum on they breath," was the reply. "They be heah in a' hour," he added nervously while I continued to scan the debris at his camp.

"What does this do?" I demanded, picking up a reflecting disk on impulse.

"Oh, that's ta signal mah people should I evah spy a ship o' they's in the sky," he explained mournfully.

"Let's take it and hide in the jungle until your reprobate 'friends' disappear," I suggested. "Tell them there were no survivors, and we can get a lift home with your people when they come."

While Jacob took a more prosaic item--a fishing pole-- we dashed into the jungle. Later we spied on Nathan while he met with the brigands on the beach, and we saw him shrug and gesticulate to indicate barrenness. They weren't happy, but they hoisted up the skull and crossbones and left the island again.

We survived by fishing and eating local plant life, and we saw many ships come and go. When there were survivors, Jacob and I hid in the jungle. Nathan became our friend and, four years later, he let me signal a sky ship that crossed overhead. We joined their crew happily, as Jacob and Nathan had helped me develop a taste for the unusual, and I never saw my home again.

An Afterword to this story is on page 253.

28

DIGGITY ISLE

by
Oliver Dolan

A blazing beam of sunshine warms Murray's neck as he regains consciousness, finding himself face down in blazing hot sand as images of the crash swirl through his mind. He manages to get to his feet, but the sudden motion triggers stomach bile to shoot up his throat and splatter down his chest.

He recovers, squints his eyes, and examines the desolate island he's been thrust upon, finding shards of glass and twisted metal scattered about the picturesque shore; an oxymoron, he thinks. He notices six long hollow tree trunks laid flat on the sand, forming the shape of an instrument he played as a child. While continuing to take in this new territory, he sees a few strands of red hair flutter up in the wind, sneaking out from underneath the destruction.

"Faye?!" he shouts. "Is that you?" His heart skips a beat as he sprints over to aid his precious sister, realizing she's the only other survivor.

"Murray?" Faye mutters. "Are we alive?"

"Yeah, I think we are. We might be the only ones who made it. Are you okay?"

"Uh… I'm not sure, everything's pretty hazy, and I can barely think… where are we?"

He lifts her fragile body from the wreckage and tells her that they're probably on an isolated island somewhere in the Caribbean. He tries to set her on her feet, but she immediately collapses back down on the sand.

"Oh no! Murray!" Faye says as tears begin streaming down her sunburnt cheeks. "My legs don't work anymore!"

Before he has a chance to respond, a powerful gust of wind blows in, causing a simple, beautiful, melody to sound from the instrument-shaped trees. As they look toward the ocean, they see that the same gust is blowing in a great black ship.

"I think they're coming to rescue us Murr! They'll be here in no time and bring us home!"

Sweat trickles down Murray's brow, and although appearing confident to his young sister, he's a little afraid of what (and who) the ship might be carrying.

***

As a dinghy pulls up on shore, a tan-skinned, shirtless man donning a gigantic black hat appears. He fearlessly jumps out the small boat, landing firmly on the beach.

"Ahoy mates!" he exclaims. "Appears you two are in some deeeeep doo-doo down here on Diggity Isle! Fear not my friends, Happy Harry's here to help!" He swiftly removes his hat and beautiful blonde locks pour down, falling halfway down his back. He looks at Murray and their eyes fixate on one another's. Murray looks deep into the shipman's emerald eyes, convinced he's the most handsome man he's ever seen, and the mysterious man briefly matches his gaze. Harry quickly switches his attention to Faye.

"And you, my little red haired princess! Aren't you a tiny treasurable treat! Can you stand or were your poor little bitty legs damaged in the crash?" He walks toward Faye. Murray tries to stop him, but Harry glides past and gets down on a knee next to Faye.

Crying again, she says, "I can't feel them at all!"

"What's your name little lady?"

She catches a whiff of his breath and it reminds her of when Dad would drink rum and Coke on Friday nights after work. "Faye," she says.

"Oh, Faye, Faithful Fun and Funky Faye, do let me take you on to my ship and fix your little limbs! And dear mister Faye's brother... your name is...? Would you let me do so?"

"You can call me Murray. And yes, but I'm coming too," he says sternly.

"Murray, Mighty Muscular and Manly Murray! You don't understand... I need to perform the Meditative Magic of the Mediterranean on precious Faye here. Using my antidote with you on the boat would make your soul float. In other words, you would die!"

"Well... uhm, okay. Just don't leave the shore and don't take too long. And... by the way... is there any chance you could give us a lift back to the United States? I have a couple hundred bucks there I could give you... we can't survive out here on our own."

Harry softly winks at Murray, then grabs Faye and dashes to his boat, climbing up a rope ladder, then rolling it up behind them.

She looks down and sees three little girls tied up with their mouths taped shut, their eyes full of fear and sorrow. Faye screams as Harry opens a hatch on his deck.

Terrified, Murray rushes towards the ship and fails to climb up its side, being nowhere strong or agile enough to scale the ship.

Harry laughs loudly then screams, "SOOOO LONG MINDLESS MURRRRRAAAAYYYY - here's a jar of rum for you to drown in your sorrows! TA-TA AND FAREWELL, AND BY THE WAY YOU SMELL!!!"

***

"Murray! Murray! My marvelous, man-ly Murrrrray!" Mom's voice sings in my bedroom.

Murray hears Mom's comforting song and begins to open his eyes... what a terrible dream!

An Afterword to this story is on page 254.

29

BUCCANEER DAYS

by
Shelly Heskett Harris

Before we begin our story, there are a couple of things you may or may not know about Texas. When you think of Texas, cowboys and Indians come to mind. However, some of the bloodiest battles were fought in the waters of the Gulf of Mexico. These attacks, usually against Spanish ships, other merchants and settlements in the area, were waged during the 1600s under the flag of the Jolly Roger.

To commemorate this colorful time in the history of the state every year, the City of Corpus Christi stages a reenactment of the city being captured by dangerous privateers.

But these thieves are actually hired by the city to help celebrate Buccaneer Days – the opening days of the summer beach season in Corpus Christi.

Today the Buccaneers sail in, capture the mayor and force him to walk the plank as he announces the arrival of the Buccaneer Days festivities.

Now we have one another Texas characteristic before we begin our story.

There are two forms of greeting in Texas, the first, "Did 'ya get any rain?" and the second, "How 'bout them

Cowboys?" referring to the Dallas pro-football team. Texans love their football and take it very seriously.

Now we begin the story of Marylynn and Ruby, bounty hunters from Frio County. We find them in Ruby's baby-blue convertible; top down, their dyed-blond hair loose and blowing in the wind. Marylynn has her feet crossed on the dashboard, and both are singing with the radio.

***

"First thing I'm doing is getting a cold beer," Ruby said. "My mouth's dry."

"Quit singing in the wind," Marylynn said. "How long you think it'll take to find this kid?"

"He's one of the Buccaneers so he'll be in costume. They'll hang out at the Cabbagehead Hotel… in the bar… we'll pick him up there, piece a cake."

"Stupid name for a hotel."

"You know… the jellyfish. Anyway, I can't believe our good luck. Going to Corpus for Buccaneer Days and getting paid for it."

They checked in to the Cabbagehead and noted the lobby and lobby bar were full of bearded men with patches over one eye and wearing three corner hats.

They had a picture of John Micheal Jones; a good-looking seventeen-year old who had matured early and was making a name for himself as quarterback on the Obama 4-A High School team.

"He's a clean-cut looking kid. How come we're after him?" Ruby said.

"Don't know. Says *robbery* on the warrant," Marylynn answered. "Do we contact the locals?"

"Gonna have to if we need to stow the kid overnight."

"Speak of the devil." Marylynn pointed with her chin at John Micheal himself walking in the door. Both women stood slowly and circled, one on the right, other on the left.

They locked the boy's arms behind his back and held tight, even against his youthful strength.

A deputy sheriff magically appeared. "What the hell's going on?"

Identification papers and warrants were exchanged. The deputy said they'd be happy to keep the kid. "In fact, I'll take him now, and you girls can enjoy the festivities."

"How's that for nice?" Ruby said, "What'll we do first?"

The two of them spent the afternoon flirting with the buccaneers and consuming a steady stream of complimentary beers sent to their table. Archie and Dale were the most vigorous of their suitors and treated them to dinner. Then found them a perfect spot to watch the reenactment.

Perched atop the bleachers comfortable and content, they settled in to watch the Mayor of Corpus Christi walk the plank.

That's when they saw John Micheal Jones, still in costume performing his roll in the pageant. Instantly sober the two crawled over people down to the ground, ducked under a no trespassing tape, and made it to the dock.

John Micheal saw them coming, jumped ship, and swam to the opposite dock.

"Wait a minute, I'm too full of shrimp to chase him!"

Ruby yelled.

"Ok. You go find the deputy and find out what's happened!" Marylynn yelled back, kicking off her shoes for better traction in the sand. She wasn't what you'd call athletic looking, but once she got her long legs churning in rhythm, it was a symphony of motion.

John Micheal could hear her coming up behind him. He remembered how easily the two women subdued him earlier. He was beaten even before Marylynn lunged and knocked him to the ground.

Ruby, with the deputy in tow, tossed her partner's shoes to her and turned to the deputy who was berating John Micheal for taking part in the reenactment.

"I told you to go home, stay there, lay low. What part of that didn't you understand?" the deputy asked John Michael.

"I don't know, coach," John Michael said. "I figured I was in disguise."

"Coach?" Ruby said.

"Well, yes?" Deputy Ed said.

Ruby and Marylynn exchanged looks and spoke in unison. "This better be good."

"We're a new school lacking in school spirit. It's been a tough year. One thing that could bring it together would be going to state in football." Deputy Ed's voice quickened as he described how team spirit would bring the student body together. "This kid is good enough to take us all the way."

"We can't just let him go," Ruby said. "Couldn't you work something out with the judge?"

"We did," Deputy Ed said.

"Well?" Ruby asked.

Deputy Coach Ed looked down, dug his toe in the sand, cleared his throat, and mumbled something.

"What?" Marylynn asked.

Coach Ed looked like he was in physical pain. "I said the kid's a kleptomaniac. We gotta watch him 24/7."

And that's why Ruby and Marylynn were waiting outside the Obama High School football team dressing room the year they won state.

An Afterword to this story is on page 255.

30

A SHIP OUT OF TIME

by
Rebecca Lacy

Roget Valle was thirteen years old when he was orphaned. Alone, homeless and with no means of support, the boy quickly saw that his best option for survival was to join the crew of one of the brigantines that called Nassau home.

Over the years, more than a few men aboard those ships had found pleasure with his mother, including Captain Leander of the *Coeur Noir*. Seeing Roget's winning smile and affable nature, the captain wanted to believe the lad was a product of his loins, and so, invited him to join the crew of one of the most notorious ships that ever terrorized the seas.

In the six years following his maiden voyage, Roget had grown into a man admired by his fellow crewmates. In addition to his prowess with the sword, he possessed a sixth sense for treasure that had greatly increased the crew's prosperity.

After leading a lucrative raid on a merchant ship, there was many a tankard of rum raised in Roget's honor. However, amidst the drunken camaraderie, a furious storm arose, and a monster wave crashed down on the ship like the hand of God, sending all on board to a watery grave. All, that is, except Roget.

As he bobbed in the water on the brink of unconsciousness, he caught a glimpse of a towering white ship on the horizon. Then, in the last moment before darkness descended upon him, an enormous silver bird soared above him. Had they been sent to exact punishment on the sinners of the *Coeur Noir*?

The next thing that Roget knew, there was a voice coming to him as though through a fog saying, "Wake up!" A slap on his face dispelled the last traces of unconsciousness.

"Are you an angel?" he asked fearfully as he tried to make out the face hovering above him.

"Hardly."

He struggled to sit up so he could get a better look at the person who had spoken. It was a girl of about his age. The bare skin her clothing reveled suggested to Roget she had an occupation similar to that of his mother.

"My name is Kaitlin. I'm glad you're okay. Hey, are you an entertainer on the ship?"

"Entertainer?"

"Since you're dressed like Jack Sparrow, I figured you must be in one of the shows."

Ignoring what sounded like nonsense, Roget asked, "Do you live here?"

"Don't be silly. I got washed overboard same as you. I pulled you to shore. Don't you remember what happened?"

"Certainly," Roget responded. "A wave capsized the *Coeur Noir*, then I saw a miraculous vessel on the horizon, and a strange bird which did not flap its wings flying above me."

"I don't know what the *Coeur Noir* is…"

"It is my ship. We must search for my crewmates," he exclaimed, jumping to his feet, and quickly collapsing as dizziness overcame him.

"Just sit still. You almost drowned, you know. Besides, I already looked around, and all I found was that old crate," she said, pointing to a chest Roget hadn't noticed earlier. "Why did you call our ship *Coeur Noir*?"

"It is not *our* ship because you, madam, were not aboard."

"You must have a concussion because our ship is the *Sea-Fari*. We're on a 7-day cruise, and when we got inside the Bermuda Triangle, all hell broke loose. Oh, and the *strange bird* you saw was probably a search plane." Seeing the question in Roget's eyes, Kaitlin held out her arms like wings. "You know - airplane?"

Perplexed that Roget didn't seem to know what an airplane was, Kaitlin asked jokingly, "Jeez, what year are you from?"

"1705, of course."

After the initial shock wore off, she responded, "Welcome to the *Twilight Zone*, dude."

Kaitlin took it on faith that Roget really was a castaway from another time. Filled with excitement, she set out to explain the modern age – all of which made his head spin. He was, however, pleased to learn that she was not a lady of the evening, but rather a *college student on spring break*, whatever that meant.

After a few fitful hours of sleep, the two awoke to a ruby-red dawn. Scanning the horizon, Roget was increasingly unsettled. "We must get to higher ground."

"Great idea!" Kaitlin agreed. "It will be easier for rescuers to see our fire."

"The ship that comes may not want to rescue us."

"What are you talking about?"

Pointing to the cask, Roget explained, "That holds treasure the *Coeur Noir* liberated from the *Newcastle*, a ship belonging to the East India Company. The captain would, I think, very much like to get it back, and not object to killing us in the process."

"Are you for real?"

"I don't know what that means, but I think the answer is *yes*."

They struggled to move the chest to the top of a hill where the panoramic view would allow them to see a ship approaching from any direction. For the next four days they took turns keeping vigil while learning more about one another and the times in which each lived.

"What will you do when the rescuers come?" asked Kaitlin.

"What choice do I have?"

"Don't worry. I'll teach you everything you need to know about the 21st century," she offered with enthusiastic optimism.

On the fifth day, a rescue party came ashore and found the castaways. Surprised, they found two rather than just the one for whom they had been searching.

Once aboard, Roget was overwhelmed by the wonders

he saw. However, just as he was starting to feel confident that he had indeed left the treacherous past behind, there arose in the distance a sight that cause his breath to catch in his throat. His hand instinctively reached for the sword that had once hung at his side. It was the *Newcastle*—a strong wind in her sails, making directly for the rescue boat.

An Afterword to this story is on page 256.

3 1

ADRIFT

by
Robert A. Strobel

A lone man sits in an empty longboat without a stitch of cloth on his back. He sits in solitude as the burning sun sears into his skin, only the sound of the ocean waves rocking the vacant craft as it is tossed amongst the waves. Not a bump of land is in sight. He is a big man, a large golden hoop dangles from his left ear. A black circular patch covers his right eye, his graying black hair is tangled in dreads that frames a fierce countenance. His beard is full and peppered with gray, and a hook is attached to his right arm.

An albatross lands upon the bow of the boat as it rocks upon the waves. A shark's dorsal fin circles the solitude shore boat as it drifts along in the open sea. He looks at the shark fin encompassing him, a cloud gray mass easing towards him. He stands and shouts, "So, we meet again. Ye took me hand! Now what be ye after?" He says, near naked in a fit of pseudo anger at this monster in the sea. The albatross cocks its head as if it is confused.

"The continual beating of this blinding sun is relentless upon me brow. I thirst for drink! Me belly grumbles for meat. A world of water surrounds me, and yet I remain parched," says the castaway as he watches the fin of the shark edging closer around the boat. The castaway begins to tell his tale to the bird.

"Me number-one was a spry fellow by name of William Seward. We called him Willy. He was an enterprising first-mate to say the least. After all, he now has me boat and set me adrift," says the Captain in a resolute manner.

The bird raises its wings in seeming confirmation.

"After we had sailed for two weeks upon the seas, we happened upon three of His Majesty's ships cruising the waters going to Spain."

* * *

"Hoist the Jolly Roger," I shouted to my boatswain. "Fire the forward cannons, batten down the hatches! Shiver me timbers. Prepare to board her!" These were me commands to the crew as we prepared to battle against three ships.

Cannon-fire was horrendous. Two of the ships sank. We secured our hold upon the treasure trove that awaited us. We boarded the lead ship in swift fashion. A young man brandishing a sword swung from the yardarm in an attempt to thwart Mr. Seward. I quickly dispatched him with me pistol. Then he fell into the briny deep.

"It's off to Davey Jones' locker with ye!" I said. Me first-mate had gone below in search of what was contained in her hold.

There he discovered a bevy of beauties. Among them was their governess, an immensely large woman with an angry scowl upon her face with a voice to match. This woman was dressed in a blue frock and a matronly white apron that covered her ample front. I had just entered the room where Willy was informing the governess of their predicament.

She exploded into me mate's face, "My name is Mildred Wallace. These girls are in my charge. I am responsible for their welfare. I demand that you sail this vessel to Madrid. We are to be presented before King Ferdinand of Spain for the Festival of Flowers, and if you refuse I shall see to it that you are put into the stocks," announced this behemoth of a woman.

"Madame, I assure you, I have no intention of harming you or your charges, nor do I have any intention of delivering you to Madrid, and ye be me hostages," I explained to this sea-cow wit me one eye cocked. "And we shan't be bringing damaged goods to the auction in Madagascar."

Upon hearing me speech, me number-one turned to me and spoke, "Captain, me Captain, these ladies have done you no disservice. There is no cause for you to waylay their journey to Spain."

It seems too, that me crew had bad blood on again me. They began to draw their weapons. I looked around to see me boatswain Cockeye Jim unsheathing his saber and bringing it to the ready. Me tiller-man had taken his knife from its scabbard and swung it, striking a sack of grain that was in the store. Me cook, Malcolm, was just on the other side, holding his frying pan in his raised hand.

I became enraged with the insolence of my crew in questioning me authority. I took me hand and latched upon his blouse and pulled him over to my face. I put the tip of my hook into his lughole and said, "Have you no fear, number-one? I'll cut you from ear to ear, you scurvy mongrel. You are to carryout my orders and only mine!" The words spat from my lips into his face. He jerked back tearing his ear, blood streamed from the wound. He pushed me away, and he pushed one of the crew. I believe it was Malcolm the cook who had struck me in me noggin. Next thing that I knew, I woke up here, a bloody castaway set adrift by my murderous group of ungrateful mutineers.

* * *

The lone man speaks his words to a swimming fin as it circles ever closer to the watercraft, bumping into his boat jostling it.

"Come and get me, you fiend," the man says shaking his fist at the huge swimming villain.

At saying this, the captain looks over the vast vacant watery mass, seeing the billowing sails of a watercraft. He cries, "A ship by all is done!"

As the ship nears his lonely craft, the captain sees that it is flying the flag of the King of Spain.

An Afterword to this story is on page 257.

32

MIGRATING ISN'T STEALING

by
JD Mitchell

For a region of outer space crowded with objects, the cold blue world kept its orbit crystal clear. There was silence after the storm passed, almost down to perfection. Nothing stirred. Nothing tumbled in place or out of it. Just a big blue giant sphere hung in the distance, with still life and small moons, dusty and crater swept, dots against the whirlwind wrapping an icy world they orbited.

The light comet-frigate *Rio Bravo* emerged from a subatomic fusion plume and slowed to a sub-light crawl. A distant sun's light reflected off the ship's pitch-black skin, a circle of orange made hazy by suspended fields of dust in the near depth of field. Without warning, the ship receded into the fugue of black stars. Only the irregular shape of whip antennae, sensory spines, and fuel-bulbs interrupted the faraway vistas of galactic clusters. The comet-frigate was a dagger in the side of the stellar darkness, driving deep into fathoms of eternity's night.

Inside the *Rio Bravo*, the crew swam on a dimly lit command bridge harmonized by old machines and lacquered panwood. There was no direction, no up and down, and activity went in all directions.

A temporary center did exist however.

All-hands-and-feet-on-deck danced around an undulation of black robes and hair. A woman's face poked out. Perfect eyebrows crowned hazel eyes above sharp cheekbones and wicked lips.

Mama-Captain of the pirate vessel *Rio Bravo* held a guidebook close to her robes. Just one more second. Finished, she tossed the book away. Her throat scratched heavy as she spoke to the crew.

"Bring me Click and Clack, the sailors from the Medicean wreck."

The crew swam upon her command, and in seconds, two men, tattooed head-to-foot, were towed to her suspended feet. Mama-Captain pulled her robes tighter around her, and the crew gathered around. She looked down at the shackled sailors of the *Medicean Star League*.

"Now comes the time when your bargain is kept, or you'll be proved nothing but a bag of lies, tossed into the airlock, hurled into a nether void."

The tallest of the two, Click, crowned by short light roiling hair, stepped to the proverbial mic.

"We can't be ransomed! The fleet command doesn't negotiate with pirates! Soon, the greatest number of…"

A swift bejeweled hand from Mama-Captain raised up high, and his defiance changed into sullen lips. Her power rose upward in glee, and Mama-Captain drank it up. "You do me a great honor, Abyssinian, with the title of pirate! But it's nothing, really, but a pointed insult. And I detest your superiors, I really do. Look around! We're after more than a few golden doubloons." She slapped a silver-ringed hand down against a cold ledge, her bracelets jingled in the chill, and her crew, the races of the Othering, laughed in unison but with each voice distinct, angry, and vengeful.

The shortest Medicean captive, Clack, floated closer to Mama-Captain. "We know, better, than to ignore what you're trying to...achieve...out here...among..."

Her hazel eyes flashed beneath dark eyebrows grown wide, and she drew back, then closer to intimidate loud in his ear. "Be careful of the words you choose, star sailor!"

The shorter of the two Mediceans looked toward his taller colleague, pleading with a healthy dose of fear, but measured by a heady calm. "I was only going to say we know that your grievances are great, since the Othering and all that, and we will do whatever we can to help your...revolution."

Mama-Captain hovered closer, speaking a soft threat. "I tell everyone to stay outta my way or you'll suffer my wrath."

The taller of the Mediceans clicked in, his defiance, refreshed and newly returned. "We are trained to die if need be at the hands of pirates like you! We won't betray the capital fleets!"

Short Clack lashed out in desperation. "You fool! Shut your mouth! That's not what she means! We just have to give her...ransom...so she can fund her...revolution. Your revolution is coming, right? Soon, the Horde will fall sunward upon the inner system. Saturn will fall! Jupiter and his worlds -- our Galilean home - will suffer! Even the Martian home world of Gnostic Ares will feel your wrath."

Mama-Captain pushed him. "You ignorant waste of cosmic dust! Nothing, not even the capital, can stop us from returning to our homes. The migration is already happening. That's, truly, the rebellious act. Warships? They're fine. But the unrestricted flow of migration? That's the challenge to the empire your Medicean fleets serve. And the rebellion is already happening."

The shorter one spoke through a quivering lower jaw. "Then…why did you rescue us? What do you want from us? Why did you bring us back to Neptune?"

Mama-Captain floated away. Her words stayed however. "A revolution without love isn't a revolution worth fighting. There's a person in the wreck of the *Crispus Attucks*. I want you to go find him. And, while love won't prevent people from dying, it might be the only way we end up winning what's ours."

The smaller of the two squeaked in pursuit of her. "Which is what?"

Mama-Captain only had words for herself. But they were words flowing over to the entire crew of the *Rio Bravo*.

"Migrating back home!"

An Afterword to this story is on page 258.

33

REMINISCING

by
A.L. Scott

The rhythmic rolling of the waves against the hull and the clock's constant tick-tocking lulled Robert into a hypnotic trance. He flicked absentmindedly at the tiny white pearl with his nail, his thoughts lost in another place. An unexpected creaking snapped him and his consciousness back together, and lifting the trinket to his lips, he gave it a good crack between his teeth.

Felt real.

Robert clipped the earring on and continued his preparations with renewed haste. The ribbons on the cuffs of his ruffled shirt always gave him trouble, as did his waistcoat.

Trouble. Just like the old days.

Robert wondered what today's gathering would bring. So many of them had not seen each other in over a decade and so much had happened in that time. The balance of power had tipped repeatedly as old hands made way for the new. It had always been about the loot, of course, it's just that nowadays there was ever more competition.

He sighed as he pulled on his brown breeches and studded wide-buckle belt, then roughly tucked in his shirt.

He swung on his crimson sash and grinned wickedly, remembering the last time he'd worn it.

The gang had sailed into their first port of call, Old O'Riley's. Everyone was in good form and up for some action. The game had them all on fire, while the rum was flowing freely. Just how many he threw back that night, Robert couldn't be sure. What he did remember was that the drunker he got, the better his wooing ability became. He must have pulled at least four times, and his mates affectionately dubbed him the ladies' scoundrel on account of that night. He, of course, took it all in his stride; he always did have an eye for a goodly woman.

Robert smiled devilishly to himself as he hoicked on his leather thigh-highs and gave his bottle a swig. Tonight would be rowdy at the very least, and that was fine with him. Life had dealt him a sullen blow of late, and he was ready to fly the black once again if need be, in fact, he hoped it would come to that.

Looking in the mirror, a haggard yet not unhandsome middle-aged man stared back at him. His stubbly jaw was wide and his eyes were bright faceted sapphires. His wild jet hair was pulled into a tight pony, which revealed only a hint of his true age at his temples. Years in the elements had hardened his physique so that he was now sitting comfortably between brute and privileged.

Many a brawl had he fought as a lad and then as a man, over power, plunder and even pittance, with war wounds worthy of a brag. But never had his very breath been sucked out of him so vehemently as when he'd laid eyes on the raven-haired, wine-pouted Marisa for the first time. She'd be there too tonight, perhaps. Perhaps tonight he might for the first time lower his defenses. Robert stood dazed for a long moment. The blasted woman was turning him into a right dandy.

And that will certainly not do.

Taking another swig, he reached for his doublet, flinging it over his broad shoulders in one fell practiced motion. Over went his baldric, followed by his faded bandana.

He recalled a final score he sought to settle with long-standing mate Hardy, and figured that the charts all pointed towards tonight favourably. The man, although a grunt, claimed not a wit to his name, and Robert felt satisfied that he'd close his eyes a richer man. Slipping his prized jewels on his fingers, he continued to drape a weighty gold chain about his neck. He'd relax to the night's revelry after first taking care of business, he reckoned. And if Hardy fancied squaring up via endless rounds tonight, so be it.

He positioned his tri-cornered hat before checking his cutlass, dagger and pistol were in place. A final glance at his reflection and a swig for stamina saw him finally through the door and into the evening.

Two minutes later he was back in his cabin room aboard the cruise liner scrounging around every nook and cranny.

Where are those bloomin' rings?

Jack was going to kill him for sure. His oldest pal was getting married a la swashbuckling style in a little under two hours, and Jack's best man, Robert, was responsible for the rings. Robert stood flustered and perplexed in front of the mirror, scratching his head.

A sudden glint caught his eye and he lowered his arm to reveal his matrimonially-festooned fingers.

An Afterword to this story is on page 259.

34

THE WRECK OF THE *CONARY*

by
D. B. Martin

Sunlight brought in a new day. I raised my head and gazed out at the horizon, perfect and empty. I was alive; the only one apparently in which I felt no disgrace. I was breathing, and that was what was important. It had been a barmy night, and the storm had been the worst I could remember. For anyone to survive, it was a miracle. But for me, my survival showed how tough I am. It took everything I had to will my muscles to motion.

The *Conary* had been a stout ship, but God and the reef had made her show her worth. She lay heavy in the water with the stores and bounty, which we had taken from the Spanish frigate *Burlandin*. They said she couldn't be taken with her forty-four guns, but we showed them. I stood on what was left.

Turning, I found myself only maybe a hundred feet or so from the shore. A gull screamed as it flew overhead while I stood alone, absorbing the fact that everything was gone—all the gold and even all the jewels to Davey's locker—gone. Overlooking I could see the ship's timber had run abroad on a coral reef, and now it was surrounded by floating debris and stores. I checked myself. I had my pistol, but my powder was wet and useless. All I had for defense was a short poniard and my marlin spike. My sword I had left below. I surveyed the waves moving in around me as I jumped into the water and made my way to the sand. Little to nothing advantageous had washed ashore—some broken crates, some timber, and the moon sail were the lot. I gazed out wondering if anyone else was alive, but nothing rose above the breaking tide.

I remember there had been a beautiful lamenting song in the storm, a song that had carried through the gale. It was so alluring, so sweet, so delicate, and filled with so much melancholy that, I'll admit, it drew us into the shore. This coastline, though I must add, we did not see nor did we know it existed. There wasn't supposed to be any island in this part of the Caribbean, which meant that this one was most likely and unfortunately uncharted. Searching next to a reef, I found a barrel of rum. *Thanks be to the gods.* I pulled it from the water, and she was full. I sat on the shore and began tapping the barrel. *What now? I'm not one to do nothing.* I had been there only moments and already felt like I was floating around with no anchor and no focal point.

Suddenly I heard a familiar voice behind me. It was Tom Bitter, a boatswain's mate from the *Conary*, rising from the foliage.

"I thought I was alone. Mighty good to see you, Gideon," Tom announced as he dropped to the shore beside me. Looking out at the horizon, a mist was beginning to build out at sea.

"What do you say? Another storm, Tom?" I inquired.

"Yeah, maybe so. Nothing like last night though," he said, rising to tilt the barrel. I watched as more went into the sand than in his mouth.

"Watch it, will you? That's a lot!" I yelled.

Looking back toward the sea, the mist was growing, quickly thicker and thicker, swiftly closing the gap between it and the island. We rose to our feet, watching this strange occurrence that no longer looked like a storm.

"What is it?" Tom said as long thin tendrils of mist slowly began to flourish and whirl above and across the sand. The horizon was gone, lost within the denseness of the billowing mist. It seemed like it was alive the way that it glided and curlicued around us.

"What the... Tom look!" I said, pointing toward the mist.

Tom turned and there in front of us deep within the mist, a grey shadow began to darken. It became larger and darker until it became almost completely clear as the mist receded from its bounds. It was a ship, a frigate no less, and a big one too, with her name clear and bold across her broadside—*The Queen Anne's Revenge*. But that's impossible! She was supposed to have gone down twelve years ago off the Carolina coast in the Americas. Then a flat-bottomed bateau appeared from the mist, carrying two oarsmen and one other darkly figure. The skiff slid a sharp end against the sand.

The chaos of life is a wondrous thing that captures the casual observer. It was in this moment when he appeared. He stepped from the vessel boldly dressed in full corsair attire. Bristles roughly braided reached down across his broad but precursive figure. His pinnacle hat, black as sackcloth, had a skull and bones embroidered white across the front. His long buttoned coat was adorned with two sets of flintlocks and cutlasses across his chest. We stood our ground, but the sight of this man caused honest reservation and questions. Could this be him? The one I had admired the entirety of my days—Edward Teach—Captain Blackbeard. It was a black day in my memory when I read of his demise.

"Landlocked are ye? Aye, be ye honest or unscrupulous buccaneers?" He said with a hollow but bold tone and a bit of swagger.

"I am what I need to be," I said without reservation.

"Aye, a bilge rat if need be, I am sure! A surprise I have you and your shipmate."

"What? Are you taking us off this island?" Tom asked.

"Take ye with me? No. We won't be sailing side by side today lad." He billowed as he reached within his coat and pulled out a scroll. He handed it to me, and I opened it.

It's a map!

"That be a map of this island," he said.

"The X?" I asked. "What is there?"

"That be yer surprise" He turned and climbed back aboard his craft.

"You can't leave us here!" Tom shouted.

"Aye, but I can, and I will. Seek and ye shall find your due surprise," he said laughing as he diluted into the mist. In only moments the bateau, his ship, and the mist were all gone.

Tom grabbed the map from me and stared at it. "What do you think it is? Did he say, *treasure*?"

"I don't know," I said, "but it is our only course. So we'll find what it is."

We spent the next two and a half days following the map. Coming upon the shore of the opposite side of the island, night was heavy upon us, so we fashioned some torches. We set them beside the location and began to dig with our hands and my poniard.

Deeper we went. We were at good man's depth when we finally hit something. It was a chest or a crate of some kind. We began to quickly uncover it. Excitement was rising in our blood. Grabbing the planks, we pulled but they wouldn't budge. We would have been in a panic if it hadn't been for the constant conversation of the treasure and what we were going to do with it. Prying at it with limbs and rocks, we beat on the box in attempts to loosen the nails. Suddenly the box burst open, throwing us back against the dirt walls we had created. There within the box lay the rotting corpse of the one I admired the most, Captain Blackbeard.

His gravid ammonia ridden body—with eye sockets in his skull blacker than any night—unexpectedly rose from the makeshift coffin. His long boney fingers reached out and pulled us both inside the coffin. Then the lid shut tight. We could hear the deafening sound of dirt filling itself back in on top of us, even over our own screams and somewhere in the blackness, a thunderous voice cried out laughing. Surprise!

An Afterword to this story is on page 260.

35

ABANDONING SHIP

by
DC Mills

Orange lights flashed all around. I could barely hear my own thoughts over the blaring of the klaxons. Smoke began to fill the air. The whole ship juddered and tilted.

'Warning,' an automated voice said.

Why are those always female? Maybe to simulate a mother's voice, I thought, *gently admonishing you to get moving.*

'Four minutes to impact.'

I struggled into my suit, fingers straining to lock the clasps sealing the helmet.

'Ninety seconds to impact.'

I had no idea where the others were. Had they even survived the explosion? I punched the button to release the air lock. Jakob appeared in my field of vision. 'Help me, man,' he groaned. I flung my arms around him trying to shield him with my slightly better protected body as the ground slammed into the ship.

***

I was lying on sandy gravel. I was alive. I tried to move my limbs, one by one. They seemed to be working.

The display in my suit flickered on. The atmospheric reading showed 18 % oxygen, 80 % nitrogen, and bits of other stuff. Nothing toxic. I unclasped my helmet and lifted it off, carefully tasting the air. A bit thin, but breathable.

I looked around me. The bulk of the barge was sitting at a distance, scarred and scorched by the rapid descent through the atmosphere and, of course, the crash. Burning debris was already fading out: not enough oxygen to keep the flames going.

I spotted Jakob lying a few metres away, not moving.

A figure approached him, a scrawny old man, limping on a badly maintained augmetic leg. On his shoulder sat an iridescent black bird. The man bent over Jakob, peering at him. He straightened with a grimace and looked over at me, still sitting in the sand.

'You fellas look like you could use a drink,' the man said without preamble. 'And a bowl of hot soup.'

I struggled to my feet and staggered over to Jakob. He was stirring and moaning. *Alive. But how badly hurt?*

'Is there a medical facility near here?' I asked the stranger.

'Medical? Now, let me see... I 'ave a first aid kit in me bunker, so I do,' he said, and his bird repeated, 'So I do! So I do!'

'He talks,' I said in surprise.

'Aye, he talks. Don't ye, Korax,' he said affectionately to the bird, who shuffled his feet and rubbed his beak against the man's stubbly cheek.

Together, we got Jakob to his feet and helped him stumble over the sand towards the bunker. A change in the light made me look up. Thick clouds were tumbling over the sky like so many dark-fleeced sheep.

'Aye,' the stranger said. 'We'd better get below afore the storm hits.'

***

Inside the bunker, I looked around me. A large console dominated the main area, with keyboards and screens and what looked like an old-fashioned holographic projector. This was a monitoring station.

'Where are we?'

'Got yerself lost, did yer?' he chuckled. 'We're on a small planet in the Ka'arib system. Nobody ever comes 'ere. Terraforming weren't much of a success, so they gave up on the place. Didn't even bother to name it. I'm John, by the way,' he added.

'Pleased to meet you, John. I'm James.'

I used the hand-held scanner in the first aid kit to assess Jakob's injuries. They weren't too bad, but he'd need a rest to recover from the bruising, so I gave him a little morphia. Meanwhile, John had provided steaming bowls of soup and glasses of a brown, sharp-smelling liquid. He was surprisingly nimble on his creaking leg.

'Come and eat,' he called, and I gladly did so. The liquid turned out to be a fluid fire by the name of Rum. Shocking, but with a pleasant after-effect.

'When the storm is over,' I said, 'I need to get back to the ship, see what's left—if I can get to the cargo.'

'What yer got there?' John asked, looking intrigued.

'Well, most of it –' I broke off as an eerie song filled the air, floating disembodied over us. 'That's the song we heard on the ship! Right before everything went awry.' I stared at the gaunt face across the table. 'Did it come from here? Did you cause the crash?'

'Please don't hurt me!' he whimpered, cowering, and I realised that I had drawn my lappistol. I took a long breath.

'The signal got stuck,' he explained. 'Sometimes it just goes like that, sending out that weird singing. I can't shut it off,' he moaned. 'I've had to listen to it every day for five years, ever since they left me here!'

I went over to the console and called up the details of the transmission. The code embedded in the musical signal was designed to disrupt the navigation systems of nearby ships, causing ambaric shorts. That's how the explosion and fire on our barge had happened.

***

A knock on the outer hatch to the bunker surprised us both. Jakob gave a start but slept on.

Outside stood a tall, handsome, and flamboyantly dressed man flanked by two brawny types. The wind, less fierce than before, whipped his long hair about him.

'Why is a raven like a writing desk?' he asked as if demanding a password, though he was the one on the outside.

'How should I bloody know,' John grumbled. The new stranger took no notice of his mood, but clasped his hands warmly. The bird on John's shoulder squawked a 'Hello!'

'So good to see you again,' he said. 'I wasn't sure you'd be alive still.'

'You could've come round earlier.'

'And who are *you*?' the newcomer asked while giving me an intense look.

'James,' I said, 'we crashed here a few hours ago. That's Jakob over there.'

'Wonderful,' he smiled. 'I'm Jack. The captain.'

'You have a ship?' I asked, stupidly.

'Of course. A clipper. Fastest there is.'

'So you're a merchant?'

Captain Jack and old John exchanged a glance I didn't quite comprehend.

'Sure, kid, a merchant.'

***

By the time the storm had settled, Jakob was coming to. After a bowl of thick soup, he perked up enough to accompany me to the wrecked barge to look for the cargo.

'Need a hand?' the captain asked. 'We've got muscle.' He indicated the silent bodyguards.

'Thanks,' I said, trying to sound casual. 'But we're just looking for personal effects. There may be bodies to bury, though,' I added, thinking of the five comrades still inside the wreckage.

'Would you mind telling me what's going on?' Jakob said, as we made our way gingerly over the debris. 'Are we trusting these people?'

I ducked a severed power line in the main hold. The ambaric systems were still functioning, at least in part. Good.

'We have to trust them. The barge isn't spaceworthy. There's no one else around. And Jack's okay,' I added.

He shook his head. 'I don't like it.'

The cargo on our barge consisted mostly of gold intended for the manufacture of nanofilaments. I put my right palm on the scanner and, simultaneously, my left eye in front of the ophthalmic scanner. Jakob did the same, mirrored, on the other side of the hatch. It slid open.

'We need to take as much as we can carry,' I said. 'Preferably without letting anyone know exactly how much we have.'

'So we don't quite trust them,' Jakob said while loading up a backpack. 'That's a relief.'

I showed a handful of the gold to the captain. 'Will this buy us a ticket out of here?'

His eyes gleamed. 'My, my, young man. However did you come across such a fortune?'

'It was part of the cargo we were carrying. Transporting gold for the manufactories on Yu'uk-Atan.'

'And they won't mind you absconding with it?'

'Absconding?'

'Well,' he said with that smile of his, 'you are abandoning your ship, enlisting on another, and handing over the valuables.'

'When you put it like that,' I said, as if hesitating, 'it does sound rather dodgy. But it can't be helped, I suppose. After all, we do have to get out of here.'

'That's my lad,' Jack exclaimed, beaming. He took the gold from my hand and slipped it into a small leather pouch hanging from his belt.

'A deal is a deal.' We sealed it with a handshake.

'Now, let's go and say goodbye to your comrades before we take off.'

***

Less than a day after we had crashed on the tiny, nameless planet, we were on our way again, on a clipper ship captained by a man who for all his gaudy clothes and bright smiles was as shady as they come. An expectant thrill ran through me.

Old John and his bird came with us, their sentence apparently served.

'Good riddance!' John said, as we watched the diminishing orb. 'Ain't coming back here, that's for sure.'

'Nevermore!' croaked the bird.

An Afterword to this story is on page 261.

36

CAPTAIN

by
Amos Parker

Standing a full two fathoms tall, the pirate captain Goregoth bellowed at his skull-and-crossboned crew.

"We draw near to restitution, mateys! We spied smoke, and so here is fire! Ready your vile and filthy selves!"

Wild and black under grey sails billowing in the cutting gale, the terrible Black Captain brandished his razor greatsword at them as if it were no more than a butcher's knife. He called her *Bonecutter*, and deep in her magical spirit she liked it.

More than fifty sets of sunken eyes watched him, from rails, deck and rigging. High above, beyond the ship's flapping black Jolly Roger with its fanged skull and white bones, racing clouds cut the Sun without spilling precious golden organs for plunder. Far below, *Bonecutter* pointed past the blue bay and to the precious island drawing near.

"I said drop anchor, corpses!"

Grumbling, the dubious crew moved, though too slow, craving gold-laden galleons over this island's plunder.

"Drop anchor, ye dogs! Drop anchor lest I rip the teeth from your jaws to bullet my twinguns and so blow your bloody brains to the wide and stormy sea!"

Grunts and creaks then filled the swaying ship, and muscular crewmen in grimy clothes and hairy chests licked tongues over the rotten contents of their mouths. They knew no tooth of theirs would survive a gunpowder blast, yet they knew Goregoth to be too full of power to bandy mere empty threats. Yet a bag of bones paled before bags of treasure.

Bonecutter's javelin tip held steady, aiming. Atop Goregoth's shoulder, his brilliant fiery phoenix glared with demon eyes about the briny ship called *Black Titan*, clacking its red beak and digging long alabaster talons deep into the muscle of shoulder. The massive man paid their bite neither mind nor blood.

"I say see!" Goregoth cried. "'Tis worthy plunder, yet you forget! The siren song my island sings has hooked another!"

The howling wind shifted and blew from shore. Weakness wafted aboard.

Ashore, a withered, white castaway stood by the bleached bones of another. Nearby, the thick smoke of a signal fire burned, clouding the air. The frail man saw awful rescue dance and sway for him on the rising tide, saw rescue from the island and perhaps from life as well. Saltwater imprisonment and its bride of thirst strangled him, yet he regretted his fire as a man might regret marriage to a succubus.

"Ahoy," called Goregoth, "unmade matey!"

"No!" cried the castaway. "I have changed my mind!" Goregoth cackled like avian thunder.

The *Black Titan* still moved shoreward. Its Black Captain noticed and, turning back toward his crew, Goregoth splintered deck wood with a stomping, booted foot.

"I lead a crew with no brains to blow! Drop anchor lest I launch your teeth to gnash off your cocks!"

Advancing on them he sheathed his sword, drew his handcannons, and with calloused thumbs cocked them hard. The crew knew their master well, and the tiny mutinous seed burned away. They grumbled, yet hauled rope, swung spars, heaved anchor chocks and released blocks as the massive anchor chain rattled and clanked like the drawbridge of a dark god. The great iron twinhook splashed down, plummeting to the deep sand of the bay and biting hard.

Nodding at last, the Black Captain shoved firearms back deep into their holster homes.

"Impressive at last, mateys. Ye and all your squirting splinters live on... for now."

The *Black Titan* swayed in the swell, a furlong from shore where that single emaciated stick of a man tottered in tatters and terror.

A stranding then seemed better, dwarfed in the sand and sea spray. He and his courage flapped in the high winds, little more than flutter and flagging bones. Falling to his knees in his rags and sandy blond hair, eyes sunken like cannon targets of the *Black Titan* herself, he covered his face in bony hands and moaned for his dead mother. She swayed before him, in his mind, like a distant rowboat on the sea.

"God help me...."

Again the Black Captain laughed like a thundering bird of prey. "Ahoy!" he boomcried. "Do not change your mind before knowing how I will change it and far more!"

Goregoth bounded to the ship rail. His full-cut black shirt billowed and his gold-buttoned vest flapping unbuttoned. Long muskyblack braids danced like cobras. He planted the balls of his giant fists on the rocks of his hips.

"Stand by, matey, to be boarded!"

The Black Captain relished the dying tendrils of doubt he felt behind him. He knew the severing of them to be the greatest amplification of command. On his shoulder, turning its head toward the crew, his phoenix flapped mighty, flaming wings. Opening its beak wide, its cry ransacked the air for miles around and far up above the crow's nest.

"Easy, Anathema," Goregoth said. "Soon enough. Soon enough."

Anathema fell silent.

The castaway fell prostrate as if near to sating his thirst with the drinking of sand. His shrieks of fear carried. The signal fire died as the Black Captain gazed at it from the rail. Wind stole and ruined its remaining column of smoke, though the castaway, face buried in grit, did not see.

"Forgive my life! Forgive it, God! I now prefer death!" The ruin of a man shrieked on, unable to stop.

The Black Captain smiled, his phoenix shuddering in flame. "Aye, but that's one chicken-hearted good morrow, matey!"

Laughter overmastered the crew. Sensing it, the phoenix seemed to steal away the castaway's piercing shriek. The castaway lost consciousness, and ears came near to bleeding. The Jolly Roger flapped high and hard on the mast in the gale, but by magic did not tear and blow away.

Again the Black Captain's greatsword rang out of its sheath. He muttered incantations, and *Bonecutter's* ringing did not die. It was the gale that died.

"You will receive me, landlubber!"

More incantations rumbled from Goregoth's sharp teeth. The wood of the *Black Titan* vibrated and hummed.

Deep water in the bay boiled. From the torrent boiled three sloop-sized razor-finned sharks. The Black Captain leapt from his ship rail to the first, sprang to the second, vaulted to the third, and at last sandsprayed with a boom to the shore. The hungry sharks sank unbidden, with evil eyes, and Goregoth frowned as they vanished.

Only the bones of the *Black Titan's* flag moved in the soft breeze then puffing. The bag of bones in the sand kept still. Far off, the crew cackled.

The cackling altered. Some vile men called out.

"Leave that corpse ashore, Captain!"

"Poor plunder it is!"

"It is broken beyond grogpower! Let the song draw in better, while we seek out a goldheavy craft of Spain."

The Black Captain turned full toward his vessel and its stormy, uncalmed laughter. Across the breech, the last boilings of the undismissed sharks faded to a water of calm. The phoenix screeched at them, hungry and flapping with full fire.

"I smell a fine soul inside," the Black Captain shouted, "Aye. Scent."

Turning back to the castaway, Goregoth knelt and clutched the bag of bones by a skullgrip and a vile hand. Lifting it from the sand, it dangled as limp as a flag flown dead and indoors. "Who were ye, that ye will not be again, dead man?"

At the words, each man of the crew remembered his past and forgot, for a time, the wealth of gold. At last the tumultuous thundercackle died.

The firebird readied. Visible between Goregoth's skullswallowing fingers, eyes bulged golden and flecked with bits of black. The Black Captain and the phoenix smelled the nearby scent of death. To the crew, the view sung of mighty death itself holding aloft the fragile essence of life.

"And who are ye that you have been drawn here?"

The castaway's sunken eyes fluttered. His travelled ship of colonists to the New World unsunk in a hallucination. In his failing mind, the pale crafts of his lost wife and children sailed away to sea and vanished in mist.

"I am nothing. I am no one's." The bag of bones took a breath. "I am yours."

With a hissing rustle of feathers and flame, Anathema snapped her beak and glowed like an earthbound star.

"Do your work," Goregoth said. "Be my hungry pet, and avast with death."

Releasing its biting talons, the phoenix flew free and high. The Black Captain and what he held did not move. Beyond the sand and to the heart of the enchanted island, palm trees grew. Before circling high over the ship, she flew low and hot over them. The silent crew watched, with recalled reverence.

At last, after Anathema's final swoop from shipward, Goregoth dropped his mighty arm and then flung the castaway skyward. The phoenix struck the man in midair, and a great ball of flames held against gravity, expanded and burned bright. The crewmen of the *Black Titan* shielded their eyes. The Black Captain did not.

At last the fire died. A charred husk fell to Earth, and as Goregoth caught it in both giant arms, as a father might catch a child, Anathema flew away, beyond the palm trees marking the heart of the island. She sang, her own song of leaving.

The smoking cinder still breathed.

"My crew!" howled the Black Captain. "Remember!"

He looked to the bay, remembering the disobedient sharks. With care he slung the human cinder across one shoulder and unsheathed *Bonecutter*. Muttering through sharp teeth, his incantation brought the sharks back, fish full of fear, and realized.

"Welcome, servants."

With mirroring leaps, he strode shipward across the creatures he'd had to call a second time. His greatsword swung hard, beheaded each and bloodying ocean. On the broad grey back of the last he stopped, sword dripping.

"You make me dishonor my blade, boneless monsters. Bring my message of obedience down to your kin with your threefold sinkings."

A last cleaving, a last leaping, and with a crack Goregoth landed on deck. "Ready the grog!" he ordered, laying the breathing cinder on hardness of oceanwet wood. "Doubt now dies."

Three among the crew dared to speak. "Worth it, Captain? Worth of mere ash? Or faith?"

The Black Captain bellowed, raging at their lack of faith, in him. "Ye forget your past!" he boomed. "Ready the grog and its flagon ye know so well! Ye shall see, though faith should already be."

A nearby crewman, shirt striped red and white on the horizontal and head bandaged, carried forward a tapered, transparent tankard. It boiled green inside, as the blue and sharky ocean had boiled before, hissing with emerald fumes and stinking of briny corruption. Bulging to half the cinder's size, the Black Captain took it in his left hand and spoke to the death on the deck. "Awake, matey. Awake and drink. The beat of life has left you, but the breath of eternity has not."

By a kind of black magic, the black cinder of a man sat up. It opened eyelids of ash, revealing gold flecked with black.

"No! Give me water!"

Cackling. Everywhere.

"Silence, children!"

The Black Captain glared at the ring of dirty men. Behind them, a deepship door loosed two whipping chains and manacles, each clanking and hungersnapping for wrists and ankles.

"Only unsalted grog," said Goregoth, smiling. "You will find no freshness in the sea. Drink to our life, or die imprisoned, to feed the waves that drive us."

The chains rattled, and the cinder took a breath. The breath cracked and crumbled like the falling frame of a house, at the end of a consuming fire.

"Will it hurt?"

"Aye," answered the Black Captain, nearer than the expectant smiles of the leering crew. "But life is hurt, matey."

The Black Captain pointed up with a giant's finger. Where he aimed, the Jolly Roger flew, as if in a cloth bag of bones, grinning. "We though, here," Goregoth finished, "are other than simple life."

The cinder of a castaway broke, as the last burned beam of that house. "Your drink, then, though I cannot move myself," the breathing black corpse said to them all. "I drink to the other. I drink to you."

The chains faltered and fell as if dead. The bowels of the ship pulled them back in, the forged iron grinding over the deck. As the door closed, sealing the chains away, the Black Captain spoke. "But I can move you, matey."

Goregoth then once more wrapped rightmost fingers around the castaway skull, lifting the body to dangle and tilting the head far back. The breathing mouth fell open, and with relish the *Black Titan's* Black Captain poured foul grog down castaway gullet, bubbling green in a river that washed not just into but over the body, hissing like hungry streams of acid.

The cinder flapped and wailed, but Goregoth held fast. Sheets of sticky blackness fell away. Swollen things broke free. The drenched, quenched castaway shuddered, and trembled, feet convulsing. Golden eyes snapped open, hands clawing air.

Every fiber of the ship waited. The red eyes of the phoenix glowed, and all souls remembered. At last the chaos ceased. The time came, and the Black Captain grinned at the golden eyes between his fingers.

"Now, matey. Plunder our admiration."

He let go, and new feet struck the deckwood.

Shuddered.

Faltered.

Balanced.

"Gold and power now, revealed soul," said Goregoth, turning to his crew. "We have grown! Gold and power grow near!"

"To gold!" echoed the crew. "To power and to more!"

The new sailor arose, smiling, sharptoothed. The crew cheered, as cleansed of doubt as their new hand was of char. The one no more a castaway studied the crew, and the Black Captain took up a muttering incantation. A hard, cold, dark wind arose with him, and in his hand the flagon filled itself with fresh, boiling grog for the bandaged one to stow away again.

Goregoth clasped the recruit's bright hand, pumping.

"Welcome, proving matey. Welcome."

Offshore, round the baypoint, a barque full of plunder hove into sight. The humbled crew knelt to its Black Captain, and then rose as the alarms and cries rang out. They, and the newborn, spread fast through the *Black Titan* and her rigging, striving hard to acquire.

"Weigh anchor, me hearties! Make there, for thy plunder!"

An Afterword to this story is on page 262.

37

BREAKING ON CAVE ISLAND

by
JZ Murdock

"Cmpmmmn. Wmmm up." Nothing, no movement. "Capmmmm, Capmmmn!" Still nothing in the cool, dark dampness.

"Captain!" Clearer now. "Wake! Up!" A stirring. The man lying unconscious on the ground, dressed in a haphazard semi-grand fashion as a somewhat confused Lord or Captain, slowly shook his head trying to recapture consciousness. As he opened his eyes, his head throbbed unrepentantly until the pain and sleep were replaced with panicked awareness.

The Captain's Lieutenant and First Mate, a pale, grizzled man in his forties named Alabaster, was shaking his head in disbelief at what had just happened. He felt great relief that his Captain Lord Ritchie was still alive. Something had—passed through the Captain. Something of vague human form and gossamer-like went right through him, just as Alabaster had grabbed his Captain to pull him to safety.

Then the thing had continued on as the captain dropped dead-like to the sandy floor. At first Alabaster had feared his Captain dead, leaving him all alone in this ghastly place.

Then he saw the captain's chest still rose and fell indicating the breath of life was still upon him.

"Wha—? What happened?" Captain Ritchie looked up into his first mate's terrified face. The torchlight flickered, which gave Alabaster's face staring down upon him a grim appearance. He looked around. Light danced on the cave walls, making the tunnel appear more of a tomb than a passage.

"You—fainted, Captain." First Mate Alabaster regretted the words as they left his mouth.

The Captain looked up at him, suddenly having a desire to be standing and slapping his first mate in the face for his words with one of his three pistols. He was fully loaded and adjusted his waist sash. "Don't be an idiot. I? Faint? Help me up ya bloody fool!"

Alabaster helped his Captain up, which wasn't a hard thing to do, for this Captain was still a strapping, young and tough. They stood there in the passage as the Captain, a Lord back home and still only in his twenties, gained his ground and solidified his statue. Ritchie adjusted his pistols, baldric and cutlass, then put his hand upon the rock wall for support. Immediately he yanked his hand back with a jerk! The rock surface felt like flesh, and it sickened him. He rubbed his hand.

"I hate this vile place!" He said in a low, controlled but too loud of a whisper and heard his own words mocking him back in trifling echoes. "What does that map show you now? You say a magician gave you this map?"

"A wizard, so he claimed. But aye, Captain. Just before I slitted his throat—gave him gills, I did—I then tossed him off into coarse waters that day, beyond our gunwale."

"How did you get the map off him? Why didn't he take it to his watery grave?"

"Well, now. I told him I would make him free, if he had anything of value to trade for his miserable life, didn't I?" Alabaster chuckled at the memory. "As I said, Captain, it claims another way out, beyond here."

"Do you really think it was wise, killing a— wizard? Who ever heard of wizards riding on ships? Whoever speaks of there even being wizards in these modern times? Outlandish." Ritchie was looking more for moments to gain composure, than in any desire to know what had happened to a wizard on their last attack. *Hmph—that cursed Spanish galleon,* thought Ritchie.

His first mate lowered his eyes, obviously thinking perhaps it hadn't been such a grand idea to kill one who claimed to possess supernatural powers.

"If we can just get far enough from our pursuers," Ritchie said, "if we can get to the other side of this fortunate island, I know another captain that enjoys using a natural harbor there. We can be safe, if we can just get to his security. If we hadn't been so close to this place, surely we would all have met a watery expiration."

"Aye, Captain. I'll get us there. And to the devil with my bad luck in killing that bloody wizard. I'll see you survive this. Surely you've saved my wretched life enough times. Happy to return the favor." They both chuckled uneasily.

The last ship they had taken had served up great wealth, but had cursed them as well. Now more ships than they could hide from, even on the high seas, were after them. It appeared they had angered the entire Spanish navy. They couldn't understand though why this one ship was so different.

They had taken all they could hold from that ship, chests of money, crates of art, weapons, gunpowder, cannon ball, and food, and then dumped overboard anything that could be used against them. No need to fight the same ship twice now, was there? Even still, they had quickly secreted the treasure onto another island, and now only the two of them knew of its location.

"You are sure there is another way out? We have already—we have already lost too much." Ritchie hung his head in sorrow over the loss of nearly the entirety of his crew. Alabaster looked down, sharing a moment with his captain for those they had so recently lost.

"Aye, Captain. At least, I thinks so. See?" He handed the map to his captain, and they both looked up into the darkness before them, neither wanting to take the next step. Ritchie looked at the map, then his memories overwhelmed him. A mere ten of them had escaped to this island. Only eight to the cave. Three Spanish man o'war had pushed them far, finally out of the sea and onto the land. An unholy situation for any pirate, but one that could be used to their advantage by way of their secret knowledge of escape, one their pursuers had not.

"Well, lead the way, lead the way." His First Mate hefted his rapidly evaporating courage, lifted the torch high and forward, and then lifted his foot to take the first step onward. However he found that he couldn't put his foot outward another step. It just wouldn't move. Ritchie looked at the man. He had seen this old man successfully go up against several in a fight on another ship's deck. He was a superstitious man, but fearless in the face of real and physical danger.

This wasn't another man or men they were up against, though. Or even an entire navy. This was—nothing. It was nothing that was killing them. And one cannot fight, nothing. He pushed the terror down.

"Come on man, move!" Ritchie's harshly whispered words filled Alabaster with pain and fear. He turned to look back at his Captain and Richie saw the look in the man's face. The last thing his Lieutenant wanted was to let his Captain down. But the man was frozen with fear.

"Good God, man! We have got to move forward. Give me the torch!" Alabaster didn't move a muscle, sweat streamed down his face, his muscles vibrated, shaking slightly. Ritchie put his hand on his man's shoulder. He could feel they were taught, locked up. He shook the man slightly, smiled in his face, and ran his hand from shoulder down to hand.

At first he couldn't take the torch, but then laid his hand over the other's until he could feel it relax ever so slightly. He gripped the torch. Slowly, he twisted it out of the man's hand. Then with his other hand, he gently patted Alabaster's other shoulder, gripped him, shook him slightly in a binding pact of so dire a situation and shared fearful prospects.

The First Mate's face relaxed somewhat, shame overcoming his fear as he relented to his better's command. His Captain stepped by him, deeper into the cave, the entrance now a good ten minutes back from them. Ten minutes? So much had happened in so little time. He turned, facing their future and nodded for his friend and Captain to continue. Assuredly, Captain Ritchie nodded, turned, raised the torch, and then lifted his own foot to step forward.

It was then that it happened.

Out of the walls on either side came the diaphanous things. Like fine threads of silk they glimmered as they attacked Alabaster, sinking in and absorbing his flesh. The First Mate screamed in agony. Ritchie stepped back out of fear and thoughtless reaction. Then responsibility bit into his mind, and he pulled his cutlass.

Growling with anger, seeing the terror in what was left of Alabaster's eyes, Ritchie attacked the fine threads, swinging vertically as best he could in the confined space, cutting through the filaments. But it was of no use. The strands would merely reattach to themselves no matter how much he swung his sword. All he was doing was expending what little energy he had left.

Ritchie continued trying to save his First Mate and friend. As he increased slashing along either side of Alabaster's dwindling form, the strands began to attach to Ritchie's sword, climbing up to the hand guard. As it touched his hand he felt a shock, then quickly it retreated, much like he had in touching the cave wall. He stumbled back against the rock wall, exhausted. Even that relief was taken from him as he again felt the wall's gelatinous texture. He jerked himself back into the center of the passage, stepping back several feet from his Mate who was by now nearly exsanguinated.

Then, it was over. Silence roared in his ears as Ritchie stood there, alone. After a few moments, anger began to overtake him replacing his fear. His fists tightened, and he heard a crackling sound. Looking down he realized that he still had the wizard's map in his hand.

Was that why he was still alive? Why he still lived on in this unholy plane of existence because of a quirk of fate in that he had forgotten to hand back the wizard's map to his First Mate and friend of these past few years, so many past many challenges and now lost triumphs?

Ritchie was now a Captain without a ship, without a crew, alone. Standing in the silence of a haunted and lethal tunnel, he was chased by an entire nation's navy, grounded, exhausted, hungry, and in fear of his life. He watched helplessly as his last and only friend dropped to the ground, a mere bag of clothing stuffed with bones. Bones that made strange hollow sounds as they clattered and settled upon the soft, cool sands of the cave tunnel.

The threads seemed somehow meatier now. They danced in the air as if searching for more, as if the First Mate's flesh wasn't enough to satiate their starving need. Then they withdrew, receding back into the walls of the tunnel.

Ritchie slowed his breathing with some difficulty. Frantically, he looked all about himself, trying to stay as far from the tunnel walls as possible. He looked first behind him, then before him, then around again until he realized his breathing was increasing from his spinning around seeking attack. His frantic survey of this terrifying situation was increasing his fears. He forced himself to stop, to stand still and listen. All he could hear was his own heavy breathing and pounding heart.

He calmed himself, consciously trying to slow his breathing, which was hard to do for his oxygen starved lungs. He evened his breaths, slowed them down and after a few minutes where nothing had attacked him, he could slow them down even more. Now all he could hear was his own breaths of air until finally he could slow his inhalations enough that he could no longer hear even them. Silence.

He listened. Only silence. No one, nothing else was in the cave with him. He was sure of that. Still, he was sure of that even while his men were being killed, one after another. Until now, where he was alone and defenseless against unholy assailants. And still there were those outside on the island, probably tracking their footprints as he thought about it.

They would be here soon, too. He had to do something.

"Good bye, my friend," he said aloud to his fallen Lieutenant. "May we meet again in a far better place. And ten thousand curses be to wizards and their kind!"

Ritchie gathered up what was left of his courage, turned and headed into the depths of the tunnel, the torch held aloft before him. Odd that he didn't find it difficult to move beyond where they had so far travelled. He wondered about that. Then put it behind him since he had no choice now but to move forward—to head to the eventual other opening of this nasty underground tunnel.

Ritchie had walked for only about a minute when he came upon a wall. *A dead end?* Panic seized him for a moment as he wheeled around, looking everywhere, above him, kicking the ground below, for a possible trap door. There was nothing.

He stopped moving and listened. He wanted out. Claustrophobia began to suffocate him. He pushed his thoughts to speed them up. He considered his next step. What options did he have? Looking into the future as best he could, as any good Captain would, still, he saw nothing. They had been doomed all along, right from the start. Doomed by a seafaring wizard who had been killed on a ship taken by pirates.

Then it all made sense. This wasn't a treasure map. It was a dead end, literally. *A dead man's tomb.* The wizard had tricked Alabaster with his last action. Probably assuming he was dead either way, or having only this map on him and of no value to a pirate, but of great value as a method of revenge by a wizard about to die.

There was only one way out, Ritchie realized in a flash of insight. The map in some way protected its bearer, probably so that he could lead the others to their demise; then expected to drop it and thus, die by his own ignorance. There was nothing else to do, either way. He would be a shallow-pated bungler if he died like Alabaster in this accursed tomb of some kind of black magic.

Captain Ritchie took a few deep breaths, hefted his gear, and started to walk back out of the tunnel. He may now die fighting the hoard at the entrance, but he would be slouching wastrel if he died standing in this accursed malevolent darkness. Still, there might be another way.

After what seemed only seconds, he nearly stumbled upon old Alabaster's ill-fated corpse, or what was left of it. He pushed on passed him with no event. Five minutes later, he came across Louis' body and Jack's and Henry's, his boatswain, and two of his gunners, respectively. They were a sickening mess, missing most of themselves as if being slowly absorbed into the tunnel. Tentatively he stepped past the bodies, fearful he might invoke some demon, or the digestion of this tunnel, this intestine of the island.

Minutes later he nearly ran to the next set of bodies, the last of his crew. A minute later he began to see light up ahead. Running more carefully, more quietly now, he finally dropped the torch as he no longer needed it and no longer wanted to be seen by his enemies because of it. Finally he reached the mouth of the cave and stopped, listening. After a few moments, he realized he had stopped breathing completely and was becoming lightheaded. There were no sounds and less from behind him.

Slowly, he moved forward, a hand now on each of his guns with the third always held ready as backup. No one was yet at the cave entrance. It was then that he realized he had dropped the map somewhere along the line. Surely it must be somewhere nearby, or he would most certainly have ended up with the same fate as that of his crew. Then he heard the voices.

Panic crept once again up his spine. He looked around for an escape. Realizing these hunters were following their footprints in the soft sands, along the side of the cave entrance the ground was more rock like. So he stepped tentatively along the edge until he was out of the cave and could leap to the side and into the nearby foliage. Then he scrambled into the thick brush and ferns of the island's surrounding plant life.

Voices grew exponentially louder as the men burst onto the scene. There must have been about twenty of them, a Lieutenant was leading. Suddenly they became quiet and whispers and hand signals replaced shouting. Ritchie lowered his head, breathing as quietly as he could, afraid that should he look at one of them, they might feel his eyes upon them, and raise the alarm; sealing his fate at the end of a hangmen's noose.

The leader motioned forward. One by one, they all entered the cave until the last one stood guard, facing outward, watching for anyone trying to follow them. There was no question that this was a Spanish naval crew. A well-motivated one.

"Cheers, Alabaster! Good night, dear friends," he whispered to himself.

Ritchie's heart was heavy with the loss of it all—ship, crew, and confidant. Then he remembered another island and a treasure only he now knew of. Still, this would be one memory that he will never tell any of, try never to think of again, and would keep tucked deep away in his heart, forevermore.

Captain Lord Ritchie, Royal ex-patriot of his beloved Irish lands, now a pirate captain without ship or crew, sadly grimaced alone and veiled from the horrors that this new crew would shortly suffer in his absence. Silently, he melted into the tropical forest toward an unpredictable future, and a very predictable fortune.

An Afterword to this story is on page 263.

CHAPTER TWO

A LIGHT IN THE HOUSE

38

X-TREME

by
Steve Bridger

He was cradled in the loving arms of unconsciousness, safe, secure, floating in a dark limitless oblivion, soundless, far away from the world of pain. Inert, but his pulsing brain would not let him rest, would not let him surrender to the sweet siren call of warm endless sleep. Signals were sent to all parts of his body, feint calls to each nerve end demanding a response. Wake up! Wake up! Limply, his senses slowly answered. Electric probes of pins and needles washed down his body. Fingers and toes clenched and unclenched. His nose drawing in overwhelming wafts of pine, sharp pungent, natural smelling salts that stung him into awareness.

He opened his eyes to obsidian blackness, no light, total darkness. His legs and arms moved sideways and were immediately blocked. He head jerked upwards, his forehead smashing, thumping into wood drawing blood. His lungs started to pound, stale air gulped down in desperate mouthfuls. He screamed as the dreadful realisation dawned. In a mindless frenzy his fingernails clawed the wood, nails digging pine, then falling by his side snapped, broken, bloody.

168

Silence.

At first he heard a scattering of pebbles fall from above, followed by incessant spadefuls falling with a deafening weight reverberating in waves through his solid pine box. His fists smashed upwards in defiance. "I'm alive! I'm alive!" he cried, but no one was listening.

Crushing silence. Now totally paralyzed with fear.

What good would shouting do? Should he accept the inevitable or go down fighting? Then something strange happened. He felt the air in the chamber move around him, cool fresh air pumped from above began to chill his toes. His left foot found an opening to a pipe cut into the wood. Seconds later his blackness was suddenly lit by an intense pinprick of red light as a fibre optic cable and camera snaked into his nightmare. They knew he was awake. They knew he was being driven out of his mind. They knew, but they weren't finished with him yet.

A plump grey-brown body, four legs and whiskers, razor-sharp teeth and eyes that could see in the dark fell through the pipe. Then another, and another until the scratching, nuzzling rats began to lick and tear at his flesh, wriggling and jerking, intoxicated by human blood. The sound of water dripping then flowing freely down the pipe distracted them only momentarily from their gory feasting. The water rose inch by unstoppable inch. He felt the slimy snaking bodies of freshwater eels brush his face. He didn't react. He was too far gone for that. He'd retreated into a protective womb of peace. He'd given up. He lay there waiting for the end, preparing to meet his maker.

They say you see a bright light in near-death experiences. The light at the gate of heaven. His eyes stung as the searing white beam burned deep into his eyes, blinding and stinging. Then an uproar of voices a tumultuous cacophony. The side of the coffin fell outwards on greased hinges, a microphone thrust into his face. "Ladies and gentlemen, I give you the winner of X-Treme Reality."

39

RIPLEY'S MISTAKE

by
H.M. Schuldt

Ripley and I returned to an abandoned inn, remotely located at the base of Greenhorn Mountain. We wanted to walk through the halls just to prove it wasn't haunted. I parked my car next to a sign at the edge of the property: NO TRESPASSING! After a long walk toward the entrance, we read another sign in the unkempt yard: KEEP OUT! It was as if the signs tempted us to do the opposite even though the town folks said it was haunted with over a hundred ghosts of people who were hung in the stairwell between the 12th and 17th centuries. We walked around a long curved driveway, curious to see several cars parked near the rickety ole mansion.

The story was told that it was purchased in the 19th century. The McKloskey family owned and operated it as the McKloskey Inn until they each found a resting place out in the churchyard a short distance away. Later in 2006, the Crawley family, who knew nothing of the inn's history, purchased and marked it as the Crawley Inn. They too were soon added to the churchyard cemetery.

The grey daylight of vast sky above warned us that a storm was about to hit. A cool summer breeze blew in our hair, but we saw it as a reason to hurry up and get inside.

Ripley pointed to a message written on the wall next to the front door. "Hey, Farris, get a load of this! Someone wrote *IF YOU GO IN, YOU'LL NEVER COME OUT.*" I looked up and saw a newly painted sign, hung above the double doorway. It read THE WHITE LADY INN.

With a turn of the knob, I pushed open the squeaky door. The main floor looked old and spacious with high ceilings and scuffed up wood floors. Sunlight came flooding in through large windows. A broken statue head lay on the floor in a million pieces. A smoky smell lingered in the air, and I saw fresh ashes in an enormous brick fireplace. Large oak beams supported two stories above, and when I looked around, I saw several places where the walls had been recently repaired. I heard a drip coming from somewhere. Off to the right a dark figure suddenly came zooming right at me. Instinctively I put up my right arm to shield my head. It flew by, and I saw its black beady eye staring hard, memorizing my face.

Ripley waved an arm back and forth and said, "Ugh! Evil bat! I hate bats!"

"That wasn't a bat. It was a raven," I said.

Ripley looked up.

My eyes went to the ceiling and came back down. "Statue heads?"

"Painted on the ceiling?"

"Weird."

The central staircase stood out in dilapidated majesty, a series of rises, landings, and turns going up and down from the main floor. We heard a door shut. Listening with eyes wide open, we heard footsteps walking down a corridor.

Looking up, we saw a stylish young man walking down the grand staircase. "I'm so sorry for the mess. Another raven snuck in, and somehow the Edgar head is scattered into bits. Someone will clean it up as soon as possible. I'm the Doorkeeper, Judd. The rooms are not ready, but the Pub in the Woods is open. You can find it at the end of the hall. The bartender goes by the name of Captain. Downstairs is off limits until we can get it cleaned up. Welcome to the White Lady Inn." He gave a slight bow forward with a polite nod, turned around, and walked away.

"This place is opening back up?" I asked Ripley.

"Who would ever want to sleep in a place like this?" Ripley asked.

Suddenly another door shut, or perhaps it was a cupboard.

"Forget the pub, Farris," Ripley said. "Let's go check it out downstairs."

"Why do you always have to do what you're not supposed to do?" I asked.

Halfway down the wide staircase, we heard a glass break on the main level. We heard more voices down the corridor. A woman laughed and called out, "I haven't had that spirit in centuries!"

"I ordered three cases, and we're just getting started," a man's voice said. "Turn on the music. And shut the door!"

Down at the bottom of the staircase, we saw an open hall with antique furniture and strange looking treasures, figurines, old portraits, and more statues. We roamed through the collection not sure of what we were looking for. Then Ripley spotted a ray of sunlight down at the end of another hall.

"Farris, let's go see what's down there."

"Ok," I said, but we shouldn't have. The hallway led to a narrow staircase made out of metal. It felt unstable. As I have said, Ripley's tendency was to do what he was not supposed to do, so down we went. We must have been on the backside of the building, down a hill and on the edge where a slanted roof was overhead. The landing was a circular slab, covered in rocks, and the walls were stone. There wasn't much room, but one small chest sat on hard mineral aggregate. I was certain Ripley wanted to open it. The rocks were wet, and there was a large pipe coming from the wall at shoulder height where a drip of water hit a puddle on the cement.

Ripley and I studied the chest with special interest, and we held a particularly personal sense of awe pertaining to the contents. Inside this unlocked chest there was one piece of treasure, a valuable left undamaged. Ripley picked it up, and we saw the statue head of Michelangelo.

I squinted my eyes. "Why is Michelangelo's head down here?"

"Beats me," Ripley said.

All of a sudden water came pouring out of the pipe, increasing in the amount, soon covering our feet.

"We have to get out of here!" I said.

Leaving the head in the chest, we returned to the narrow metal staircase. Ripley gave it a jiggle just to see how unstable it felt. He shouldn't have done that though, because it caused the bottom half of the staircase to fold upward.

"You've got to be kidding! Help!" Ripley called out. Water rose, inching its way up our shins, and by the judge of small space we were in, it was only a matter of minutes before the water level would cover Michelangelo's head. "What is this place? A well?"

"Some kind of a man-made tower with a well at the bottom. A badly constructed man-made well. Lord, have mercy." I looked up, hoping to find a way out.

There was an opening in the roof, way up high. Lightning struck, and rain started to fall down into the well. The water level was up to our shoulders when the water had finally stopped flowing out of the pipe. We stood there with wet hair and rain splashed in our face.

Quietly, a black raven came and landed on a ledge up high in the well. Several more flew in, landing on a circular ledge. They looked at us with their beady black eyes, trying to recognize us.

"It has a rock in its beak! Watch out!" I cried.

One of the ravens opened its large beak, letting a big rock fall down into the well. Ripley tried to get out of the way, but it hit him in the head. Each one of the ravens had a rock in its beak. One by one, the ravens began to drop rocks into the well.

Ripley caught one of the rocks and threw it back up. "Stop it, you dumb birds! Enough already! We're doomed!"

A female figure silently appeared at the top of the tower. The slender woman looked down. It was none other than The White Lady.

Hundreds of ravens landed in rotation with rocks in their beaks, and the only safe place to go was underwater.

"Ripley, let's pile up the rocks underneath the staircase and stand on the chest." We held our breath as long as we could while hundreds of rock missiles landed into the narrow well. Finally it seemed as though the attack ended, and we came up for air. One last rock came down, hitting Ripley in the head.

We piled up more rocks as they sunk to the bottom. The extra height was enough to reach the folded staircase. Little by little we used the strength in our arms to pull ourselves up to the wobbly staircase. It banged against the wall. At one point, it swung open, crashing down into the water. Ripley and I soon made our way back up. Standing at the top of the rickety ole staircase, barefoot and dripping wet, we looked back on the stupendous event, frightening and fantastic, the well that almost took our last breath and the ravens that had, as it would seem, inadvertently saved our lives.

CHANGE OF FORTUNE

by
Kristen Strassel

I'd been here before. I just knew it. The Victorian seemed so familiar to me with its mismatched paint and old musty wood smell. I knew where all the rooms were without asking. I felt at home, even though it wasn't mine. It took all I had in me to not to hang my coat in the closet under the staircase then head to the kitchen at the end of the hall to make myself a cup of tea on the potbellied stove.

Instead I stood awkwardly in the doorway with my friend Maggie, peering into the sitting room that I knew was to the left, admiring the warn round rag rug still brightly colored though faded from the sun shining in through the huge windows that illuminated the room, even on this dark day.

"Take your shoes off before coming in here!" An ancient woman barked from the table in the middle of the sitting room. She erased any homey feeling the building held. Her face was shriveled and carved, likely from years of smoking and questionable decisions. And today I was going to trust her to tell me what lies ahead of me in life in return for my forty-nine dollars.

I kicked out of my chucks, ashamed that my socks didn't match. I didn't think I'd be showing them off today. Maggie slid out of her flats, her toes perfectly pedicured. Just like her to be prepared. We padded into the room and sat down, disturbing the cat that held court on one of the chairs, napping. He left the room, making sure we took note of his indignance.

"It's forty nine dollars, and gratuities are appreciated." I took the hint and slid three twenties out of my wallet, pushing them across the table. She nodded as she counted the money. I hoped my tip improved my fortune.

The woman raised a match to an antique oil lamp, intricately detailed with cherubs and vines. Again I felt as if I'd seen this lamp before, but it was so unique, there was no way. She shuffled her tarot cards carefully, and when she was satisfied with their order, she instructed me to pick one from the pile. She laid out the cards in a specific order and considered them thoughtfully. She looked from the cards to me several times, only raising her pruned finger to her lips, but not saying a word. Did this woman know what she was doing? I was beginning to feel as if I would have spent the money better if I had thrown it out the window.

"What's your name, girl?" I jumped. She almost scolded me.

"Lilly."

"Hmmm." She seemed perplexed.

"You've lived in this house before."

"No ma'am, I haven't. I've only lived in three different places my whole life."

"I'm not talking about this life, girl!" Maggie and I eyed each other, neither one of us could conceal our alarm. "Your husband…"

"I'm not married…"

"Listen to me! Your husband Abel built this house in 1893. Your name then was Mary Lillian. You bore eight children here. Your husband was not a kind man. He kept you housebound, not letting you go further than the backyard. Have you felt trapped in your current life, Lilly?"

"Well, uh." I wrenched my fingers around each other nervously in my lap. "I don't know."

"You were just complaining on the way over here about your dead end job, Lil." Maggie pointed out. I shot a look at her. I wasn't sure I wanted any confirmation this crazy old woman could possibly be right about anything in my life. "What do you want to do with your life, Lilly?"

I gulped. "I want go to Italy and finish my Masters Degree."

"Look at this card," she demanded as she tapped the middle card on the right end. "This card holds your future. It says to let go of inhibitions and do what your heart desires. You can only find true happiness when you are happy, Lilly."

I nodded. I didn't comprehend much more of my reading or any of Maggies. My head was too full of my past. Everyone knew me as a notorious homeboy. I'd felt a connection to this house immediately. And this woman picked out my misery with my chosen, or maybe not so chosen path, just by looking at a card.

I felt lighter and more optimistic than I had in years once I was free of the house that trapped me.

41

A BYGONE SPIRIT

by
Randy Dutton

Thomas sat in the wing chair, straining to see the dusty fixture hanging from the high ceiling. Its disconnected lamp cord looped around a post. Old crates, stage props, and other such artifacts crowded this dimly lit, wood-slatted storage room since the attached dance hall was condemned decades before. The experience was about to start, just as it had on every Sunday he was in town. He smiled as flickering light rays started dancing from the chandelier's dangling crystal. Within moments, he was surrounded by music from a bygone era. It never failed. The basal tones of the local big band's music originated from everywhere, and yet, nowhere...their ghostly emanation had no unique source but seemed to vibrate from the old wood beams. The loss of tonal quality created a melancholy atmosphere. He smiled.

Thomas long believed the historic building had absorbed the essence of the many retired musicians who had lived here, releasing their pent-up energy at precisely the same time. It was a secret he kept, even from his family, for fear the spirit would sense betrayal and vanish. To know magic existed strengthened his soul.

Since he had stumbled upon this magic 15 years ago, he had made this old apartment building's repository his mecca, a solace from a confusing world. His childhood phobia of failing had long since vanished, thanks to this spirit's resonance. The music replaying in his head emboldened him through his formative years and early military career.

Sensing a higher power at work, he felt favored that he'd been distinguished from others. *Perhaps it's my Calvinist upbringing that some minds are sparked by God's grace, and through his goodness, I could help others.* With this peaceful resolve, he never wavered when others claimed indifference or futility.

After half an hour, the rhythms stopped and as if on cue, the flickering light vanished. The room regained its darkness, the signal for him to return to his parents' apartment. Thomas had been deployed the past couple years. Now that he was home, they were eager to hear the details of how he earned his Silver Star. The citation read: 'In recognition of perseverance in the face of the enemy.' To him it was just another vicious firefight, a continuation of his life's mission to protect those around him.

Neighbors he'd never met were at the reception. All were retirees, most had worked at the adjoining dance hall. By the time the crowd thinned, he had formed a kinship with one octogenarian who described his own perseverance through combat by replaying music in his mind during his worst encounters.

The old veteran invited the young warrior to his apartment to talk about survival under tough circumstances. Thomas followed the shuffling man to his small room. As he entered, he was drawn to the old posters pasted to the crumbly walls. Some of the art was signed by now long gone musical dignitaries. A tarnished trombone leaned against the corner, next to a small shrine with his wedding photo. The old musician poured a couple beers, then turned on a bright spotlight that illuminated his deceased wife's portrait and the phonograph below it. The turntable's mirrored surface cast a bright beam that reflected onto a plaster crack high up the wall. "I always do this right after church," the elderly man said in a gravelly voice while removing a big band record from its cardboard sleeve. "It was my wife's favorite album from our dance hall days." Moments after the needle touched the vinyl platter Thomas recognized the music, and his eyes traced the reflective beam back to the wide crack. He smiled. The storage room was on the other side.

42

1666 WILMINGTON AVENUE

by
Harry Alexiou

Everybody on Wilmington Avenue knew the house at number 1666, but nobody wanted to go near. It was tragic what had happened three years ago, and Freddy had since become known as *the weirdo* by the local kids. The front lawn was always trimmed and edged down to perfection, the fragrant rose bushes expertly pruned. Oddly enough nobody had ever seen a gardener or the gardening in progress. The house was freshly painted every six months, but black was neither the most popular nor appealing colour scheme.

Freddy Watts entertained no visitors, took no calls, and had his weekly shopping delivered. In fact the only sign of life was the flickering lamplight from within. Freddy gently rocked back and forth in his favourite chair…it had been hers. The bottle of Jack Daniels on the beautifully polished occasional table to his right was half empty, and he eyed it with disdain. He squinted at the majestic oak veneer grandfather clock in the corner of the room and hadn't realised that it was almost that time again. *Tempus Fugit,* he thought as he carefully topped up his glass. The clock struck midnight, but the usual chime sound was replaced by the now familiar sound of beautiful magical panpipes. As their eerily mesmerizing sound filled the room, the brass lamp doubled its intensity, bathing the room in a glorious kaleidoscope of warming colour. Freddy smiled, for he knew what was coming next. Jess appeared before him with her three little helpers: Millie, Molly, and Mandy.

'We must get to work and sort this garden out, Freddy. It's a mess again,' she said.

'Yes, yes. You go on ahead. I'll just get my gardening shoes on, dear.' Freddy thought about how he couldn't manage it without their help whilst Jess and the girls ventured out to fix up the garden.

Nobody was ever seen on Wilmington Avenue after midnight, but Betty Hargreaves had been to visit a friend only five doors down and was hurriedly walking home when she spotted movement outside number 1666. She hesitated, and as she focused she could make out the figure of Mr. Watts. She'd maybe seen him once in the past year. *Poor guy… never let anybody help him*, she thought. He was talking, but there was nobody with him. Betty approached slowly and spoke in a low voice.

'Mr. Watts, are you alright?'

'Who's there?'

'It's Betty Hargreaves, I used to be Jess' jogging buddy.'

'Oh, Betty, you've caught us right in the middle of our gardening.' He stood up and looked around. 'Oh… looks like the others have gone for a break.'

'Mr. Watts…'

'Please, call me Freddy.'

'Freddy, it's one o'clock in the morning. You have to speak to somebody. You need help. They're gone... remember the accident three years ago?'

'Gone? Oh no, you're truly mistaken. Jess and the girls always help me out with the chores, especially the gardening.'

Betty could smell the drink on his breath. She sighed and placed a comforting hand on his shoulder causing him to flinch. 'It's okay' she assured him, feeling his body relax somewhat. She wondered when he'd last had human contact.

He looked at her with a vacant stare and said, 'They're gone.' He tailed off his words and looked down at the well-kept garden, 'You scared them off. That's what you did.' At that moment Betty glanced up at the house and saw the lamplight glow brighter, so bright that she had to shield her eyes, only to see it extinguished seconds later. She thought that she heard a musical melody of sorts but quickly dismissed the odd sights and sounds and turned back to Freddy.

'Freddy, you have to move on. We all miss them, but you've kept the house and garden nice all on your own. It's you, Freddy, you've persevered and kept it all going, but you need to let them go now, to let go of the past. Open up and let your friends help you to rebuild your life.' Betty pointed toward the house. 'They will be at peace if they know that you are.'

Freddy dropped to his knees and broke down, sobbing uncontrollably. His cries could be heard all along the street. After a few seconds the lights started to come on in the quiet homes of Wilmington Avenue. Residents slowly filed out toward number 1666 to where Freddy Watts knelt, finally letting go and preparing to welcome the new light of life.

43

BAZEL & THE SPIRIT CANDLE

by
Alli Vaughan

He awoke, the memory of the wind from his dream brushing through his long hair, still in his mind. It was the wind of home, the kind of air that tendriled through the friendless bush, pulling desert salt scent with it. Would he ever again feel a breeze against his face, or smell the sky fragrant with tiny crystals of home?

Not in this dead wood. Seria's house was all green things, moss-choked and fern tangled. And she had been gone for what seemed forever. Why had he made her that promise anyhow, if he was a child of sand?

"Watch the meeting home, Bazel, the home for all of us wanderers," she had said, eyes of liquid gold staring into his.

"Of course, I'm here already, and Fallon should come soon. I will stay here until then," he had replied. He had said those words because his brother Fallon promised to come from Gadara a few days after him. Fallon enjoyed the mountain air much more than his older brother Bazel ever would, and Fallon would not mind the long wait while Seria went about the world.

But Fallon had never come to offer him relief, and Seria had never come home. No one who knew this hidden cabin had showed their face. All this time he had been alone, listless and bored. And he had been afraid.

As he did every night, he stood up and strolled to the back porch, holding the spirit candle out from his shaking body, its flames melting into the darkness. It was the only way to drive off the dead.

The shrieks and sighs of the lifeless drew near the house, but the tiny candle flame repelled them back into the night. Once he heard no sound, he placed the candle in its holder. Watching the flame burn, he fell into an exhausted heap on the porch, covering his hands with his face.

Why had no one come? He sat up, his eyes traveling aimlessly. "Where are you, Fallon? How could you do this to me?"

The night creaked back, and silence followed. *A trick of light!* He thought he had seen the fire falter as if someone blew on it, but its steady flame answered his questioning gaze.

"Fallon," he cried, "you must hate your own flesh to leave one as me trapped in this green place!" Silence only. Tears streamed down his face. How worn he felt, how deeply alone. Then he heard a familiar sound, and his tears dried quickly.

The song of the spirit, three single notes, singled a new ghost entering the forest. Another dead come to walk the forest. Fallon glanced at the burning candle, hoping to see its steady glow.

Again the flames dance! He gasped at the sight. Fear beat like his own heartbeat, and he waited for a phantom to emerge from the forest growth. Only a powerful entity could withstand the spirit candle, an entity he could not hope to face alone. He held his breath as a figure drew near.

"Fallon!" He gasped at his brother's familiar face.

"Brother, I have tried many nights to come inside, but you have lit the candle in the night, driving me back into the darkness. If you will but let me in, I will take your place.

"Phantom! I don't know you anymore! Your soul is cursed, brother! Go away and stop trying to trick me!" His shouts were desperate and riddled with madness. "I will never let you in this house!"

"Oh, Bazel. What have these long days alone done to you? Don't you recognize me?"

"Tricks and lies," he shouted.

"Bazel, I am of the sand, like you. We do not deceive our own. Look at me and see that it is I, Fallon."

Bazel offered a steady gaze, no longer washed with fear. He stared many moments at the ghostly figure and then reached out and extinguished the flame. He no longer feared the dead.

44

THE RETURN

by
Christian Warren Freed

Soft winds played a haunting melody as they blew through the cracks in the house. The aged wooden planks were warped and missing paint. An old rocking chair swayed back and forth on the porch, and beside it sat an empty flower pot with a broken lantern leaning against it. Cobwebs flickered from the supports of the chair. In the distance, unseen in the night, echoed the baleful hoot of a great horned owl. Night had settled in, blanketing the world in tender embrace as the weary were granted respite from the trials of the day.

All that is but one.

The old man eased onto the porch. His tired eyes scanned the rolling hills and lightly forested fields. Wisps of stark white hair clung to his head, speckled by liver spots and fading freckles. His once sharp blue eyes were tired now, past their prime. He felt old. His body was thinner, fragile. With a heavy sigh he took his usual seat and just watched. He hoped this night would finally be different.

He'd lost track of how many years he came out to sit on his porch with that broken lantern in his lap. Decades at least. His very life seemed defined by it. He was bitter, angry at the heavens for a perceived injustice, oh, so long ago. The lantern was a constant reminder of his failure to protect his wife. A mockery of what could have been. An old promise said it would light when the time was right. He'd been waiting every night for so long and never so much as a flicker.

The old man sighed and began his nightly vigil. It wasn't long before he began to nod off. The nights were longer these days, and it was all he could do to try and stay awake.

Autumn was here. A faint chill clung to the old house. Leaves of red, yellow, and orange drifted past on the wind. Then he heard it. The subtle chime echoed over the hills and through the valleys. The old man snapped alert, his gaze automatically lowering to the lantern. His eyes widened. A spark. Small, intense, but full of life.

"Have you ever given up hope?" a voice asked.

The old man started. There, standing at the bottom of the steps was a tall figure shrouded in a cloak of blinding colors. His heart quivered. "You've come back!"

The figure took a step closer. "I have never left. Every step you've taken, every breath you've taken I have been right behind you, catching you when you lacked the strength to continue."

Tears welled. His strength threatened to abandon him. "I've missed you so much. All these years, I never dared to dream."

The other's voice softened, turning melodious. "Yet you still sat vigil, waiting for the chime. You were always a good man, Daniel."

"How could I not? You said you'd come back to me, Sara. I've been so lonely."

Sara reached up and lowered her hood. Her face was angelic, glowing with radiance that had been stolen during life. She was almost translucent and hovered just above the tickle of grass. "My dear, Daniel, my illness was never your burden to bear. I was called away to a better place. This is not the life you were meant to live."

"It's the life I chose," he defended. "I need you, Sara. Always have." She smiled, sad and warm. "Daniel, it's time to let me go. You still have a life to live, and there is much work to be done before you can join me."

No. His heart stammered. Coldness spread through his veins. "But I..."

Sara reached up and gently touched his weathered cheek. "Daniel, this is how it must be. Let me go. Live your life. We will be together soon, once your task is complete."

"Do you promise?"

She smiled again. "Always."

He closed his eyes, relishing her touch. When he opened them again she was gone, leaving him filled with new purpose and filled with warmth. The lantern flickered once and extinguished, blown out by a kiss of wind. Daniel stood on the edge of his porch staring at the spot his wife had been and for the first time in a very long time felt free.

45

BREAKING BRADY

by
Oliver Dolan

I reluctantly roll out of the comfort of my warm bed and make my way to the bathroom to brush my teeth and take a shower. It's almost noon, and I have class in an hour. My roommate, Brady, a somewhat peculiar South Carolina native, recently had his mom down to clean our place.

I walk out of our sparkling clean bathroom and into Brady's room to say good morning. His girlfriend dumped him last night, and I've hardly had a chance to talk to him about it. The first thing I notice is the Budweiser in his hand and about ten empty bottles on his nightstand. His anxiety pills are scattered all over the ground. His eyes are adrift, and he can hardly put together a sentence.

"Brady!" I exclaim. "What's going on man? It's not even 12:30, and you've already crushed a 12-pack?! How many of these have you taken?"

"Chill out man," he says. "You don't even know how this feels… I can't believe her. She's the first girl I ever dated. Don't know how she could do this to me. I don't want to go to class. Don't want to go to work. I'd rather die. Life sucks. Oh, and six, I took six of um."

"WHAT? C'mon man why'd you do that? Get a grip! She never treated you right anyway, and you can do a lot better. I'd tell you to go to class, but you're all kinds of drunk. Get some sleep, and we'll talk later."

I turn away and walk down our spiral staircase into our kitchen. As I do, guilt creeps into my stomach. *I shouldn't have been so mean – what a nasty tone I just had – he just got his heart broken*, I think to myself.

In a lot of ways, I'm happy they broke up. I had gotten sick of the rhythmic sounds coming from his bedroom when I was trying to fall asleep. They created the strongest jealously I'd ever felt, keeping me up late wondering why he had a girl and I didn't.

I come home from class, and Brady's fast asleep. Instead of going out and partaking in Thirsty Thursday, I sit down on the couch and light a candle that an old girlfriend had given me. I look deeply into the candle, kick my feet up, and begin to ponder what advice I can offer Brady to get over his ex. I think of all my previous relationships and the ways I healed my wounded heart. The candle flickers, but at some point the flame will die. Everything comes to an end at some point. College will end soon, friends become strangers, and eventually our lives will come to a close. Like it or not, you have to accept what happens and move on from the disappointing endings, and make the best of your situation with what you've got.

The next day Brady and I head up to Lake Murray and take his boat out on the water as we have many times before. I suggest we head to the lake because I know it calms him down. It eases his nerves. He's pretty quiet for most of the day, and we spend our time tending to our fishing poles, although we haven't had so much as a bite. As the sun begins to set, we look at the beautiful water and the amazing colors reflecting off of it. He looks my way with sorrow in his eyes and begins to speak.

"I still don't get it. She didn't even give me a reason. I'll probably be single for a long time now, and you know my luck with that."

"Brady, I've been dumped a time or two, and I know how it feels—the emptiness, the nothingness, the despair, the confusion. But the sun sets on those nights, just as it's setting right now, and it will rise again the next day with me knowing that I still have to go about living my life. There will be others girls, and one day I'll be looking up at the alter while you're kissing the girl of your dreams. We're seniors in college, and we only have one chance to live our life. Let's do it right."

Before I'm finished, our poles jiggle simultaneously, and we reel in two big Striped Bass. We smile and hug, and from the look in Brady's eyes, I know the flame in his heart will burn bright again soon.

46

THE STORMS OF POINT SCOTT

by
Gail Harkins

Salt spray crashed against sea stacks, hurtling salty plumes upward into sheets of rain. Will shielded his camera and took another shot of the fury battering the rocky coastline. It was transfused with raw, elemental energy – he hoped. When he finally retreated and began the trek to his campsite, the water had soaked through his rain parka.

The trail meandered through old growth cedar and spruce, ending in a wall of salal. "I don't remember that," he thought, backtracking. He wandered circuitous deer trails as the sky blackened. Through the forest, a light flickered—he followed it hopefully to a rustic cabin.

As he neared, the door opened and a middle-aged woman stepped onto the porch, hurricane lamp in hand. Her woolen skirt skimmed booted ankles, and was topped by a gray fisherman's sweater. Her graying hair was pinned neatly in a bun. "Come dry off. I've been waiting for you."

"Thanks. What do you mean, 'waiting for me'?" he asked, cautiously stepping into the cabin and peeling off his jacket.

"I saw you with that gizmo down by the rocks. These storms...." She shook her head and pointed to the camera dangling from his neck. "You a photographer?"

He shook his head. "Maybe someday. I'm waiting till I'm better."

She glanced at the door. "I'm waiting too." She handed him a cup of tea, and he placed his boots by the fire.

"You maybe passed my mister on the Point Road? Erik Johanssen, he is. I'm Tilde." She paused hopefully. "He'll be back soon. He took the wagon for supplies before the winter storms close the road."

Will shook his head. Point Road washed out fifty years ago, he knew. It was just a trail on modern maps. "I must have missed him."

She sighed. "Well then, tell me about yourself while we wait."

Will talked about his engineering job, his desire to be a professional photographer, and his fears of failure. "It doesn't make sense to give up security for what could be a pipedream."

"Maybe," she admitted. "What've you done about it?"

"I'm taking pictures..."

"Hrummph. Takes mor'en that. Take this farm. Everybody said we couldn't make a go of it, but here we are."

Tilde took a battered railroad lantern from the mantle, lit it, and left it on the table. "When ye want something badly enough, ye make it happen. Think on that awhile. The light won't bother me." She picked up her hurricane lamp and crossed the cabin to the bedroom. She turned and pointed to the trunk. "There's a blanket in there. You can sleep by the fire."

The wind howled through the night. Just before dawn, it died down. Will thought he heard singing, with tones that rang like his mother's crystal... Tilde saying, "I waited, like you said," and a deeper reply, "Goodwife, it's time we both go home."

Will rolled again, into a deep sleep. He awakened to the onslaught of rain on his tent fly, but he was warm and dry. Opening his eyes, a strange lantern sat to one side of the tent. Its globe was still warm. Will unzipped the tent and peered outside. He saw the stone fireplace where he'd dried his still-toasty boots, but the hearth was cold and the cabin was gone. Only the foundations and the encroaching forest remained. Nothing more.

He decamped that morning, stopping at the ranger station as he left.

"The old farm, eh? That's the Johanssen homestead. Sad tale. They had big dreams for the place, but the husband was swept off Point Road in the storm of 1920. The wife stayed on, trying to make a go of it till she died. 1941, I think."

Will's mind churned with suppositions in the hours it took to reach the ferry terminal. "It can't have been a dream. My boots were dry, and there's that lantern..." Gradually, he accepted the impossible.

On the ferry back to Vancouver, he reviewed his photos. "They're actually pretty good," he admitted, "and some are outstanding."

"I agree." The lady seated next to him smiled apologetically. "I looked. Where do you show your work?"

"I'm not ready."

"Ridiculous!" She withdrew a card from her valise. "This is my brother's gallery. Tell him Prairie said to make an appointment."

He phoned the next day.

Will still wonders whether he has what it takes, but soon, he thinks, he'll know. His first show, *The Storms of Point Scott*, opens next week.

47

THE HOUSE AT THE END

by
Janet Bond

Living in a big city was nice for a while, and then it became stressful. My name is Janet Jones, and I lived in a place called Hattiesburg. One day my parents decided to move to Chicago where my aunts and uncles lived. I had two other sisters, but they wanted stay in Hattiesburg with grandmother. When my dad found a good job, he bought us a cheap house. The house was very big on the outside, and it was located down at the end of a road with nothing but bushes and trees around it. The color was dark blue with windows looking like something was peeping out at you. We finally moved in and settled down.

It was peaceful for a while until one day. A lady appeared out of nowhere knocking on the door. My mom opened the door, and there stood a tall lady with dark hair and dark eyes. "Hello," she said with a smile on her face. "My name is Mrs. Jackie. I live across the field." Her voice kind of made me feel weird in my stomach.

"Hi. I'm Mrs. Jones." My mom invited her in and offered her to have a seat.

I went upstairs to my bedroom while they talked. I looked outside my window and saw a black cat standing by a tree. I went to get a piece of bread to throw to him, but he was gone when I got back.

My dad worked late at night, and he didn't make it home until early in the morning.

The lady left, and that's when I came back downstairs. My mom told me she was going out for a while. I was old enough to stay by myself.

After my mom left, I turned on the television to watch some cartoons. I must have drifted off to sleep. I heard a beating sound on the wall. It scared me. I jumped up and looked around the house. I saw Mrs. Jackie standing there looking at me with them strange looking black eyes.

I asked her in an angry voice, "How did you get in here?"

She answered, "The door was standing open, and I walked in."

I noticed she had a lamp full of oil, so I asked her, "What's with the lamp?"

"This lamp has special powers in it," she said.

My mind started racing with crazy thoughts, wondering what was she up to.

She gave the lamp a shake. Strangely enough, I saw the room change into a motel with people dressed from the 50s. They were dancing and drinking alcohol with each other. My heart almost jumped out of my chest. Mrs. Jackie told me not to be scared. She wanted to let me know what this house was like years ago. The lamp was burning bright sitting on the coffee table.

Suddenly the lamp fell on the floor. No one noticed, but me. I tried to call out to Mrs. Jackie, but she didn't pay attention. The lamp caught the papers on the table on fire. The more I hollered, the more the people danced. I ran out of the house, watching flames burn in the window. I started hollering for help, and that's when I woke up.

I was sopping wet all over, but the house was not on fire, and the television had gone off. My mom came home with some chicken for us to eat. After she cleaned up, we set down at the table. I wanted to tell my mom what happened, but I knew she wouldn't believe me. After I ate, I went to my room to relax because I had nothing to do. School was out for the summer, and I was bored already. I began to think about what I saw, and I wondered if it was really true that this house was a motel that caught on fire with people in it. I didn't understand why Mrs. Jackie couldn't hear me when I called out to her.

We had an attic that my mom had not discovered yet. I decided to go and see what was in there. I opened the door and looked inside. There were things covered up with white sheets, and it smelled like smoke.

When I pulled a sheet off, I saw a table with a lamp sitting on top of it. I thought to myself, *Is that the lamp from my dream?* I saw some old pictures with people dancing and drinking. I stood still for a minute. I started to wonder, *What if it wasn't just a dream?* I looked through more pictures, and there it was… a picture of Mrs. Jackie with a man standing at a bar, and they were serving something.

The sight of that picture made me run out the door, race downstairs, and ask my mom, "Do you know anything about this house from before we moved in?"

My mom told me, "This house used to be a motel back in the 50s. Single people came here when they wanted to party." I couldn't believe my ears when she said that.

"I saw a fire... and people dancing," I began to tell my mom.

"You sound like you're losing your mind. You couldn't have seen it because it happened before you were born," she said.

I told my mom, "Mrs. Jackie came over with a lamp in her hand. She gave it a shake, and I saw people drinking and laughing. The lamp was on the table, and it caught some papers on fire. I hollered to Mrs. Jackie, but she couldn't hear me. Mom, what happened?"

She looked at me with fearful look on her face. "Everybody in the place was burned up, even the owner and his wife."

I took my mom upstairs to show her the pictures, and to see what the room smelled like. She couldn't believe her eyes when she saw the picture of Mrs. Jackie. My mom wanted to leave right away. She called my dad, and he came home. When she told him what had happened, he said, "That must be why the house is set off by itself. If you want to leave, we can. But it is a waste to leave something cheap behind."

I couldn't wait to leave, but I would always remember the house at the end.

48

ACCOUNTING

by
Lynette White

At the defiant age of eighteen, a family vacation at the cabin was the end of civilization as I knew it. Therefore, it was the bane of my existence. I sulked around the cabin all day yesterday and today until, shortly before sunset, utter boredom finally forced me outside.

I started walking down a familiar path and as I did I remembered there was a time when I felt different here in the forest. I would become one with the trees and the animals, but somehow that was lost to me now.

As I pondered this, my feet carried me to the end of the path. Old man McGregor was our closest neighbor and a permanent resident here. When I was young I spent more time with Mr. McGregor then I did with my family. He taught me about the animals, the plants, how to navigate the forest and how to listen to the animals for signs of danger.

I knocked on the door and when there was no answer I slowly opened it. "Mr. McGregor, are you here?"

"Be there in a moment" came a muffled reply from the kitchen.

A LIGHT IN THE HOUSE

He appeared a few moments later and stopped in the doorway. "Well bless my soul, little Kerrie Jackson. Your Uncle Mike told me you guys would be up this weekend."

He pointed toward a chair. "Sit, sit child."

We settled into chairs and were discussing my plans to start college in a couple of months when a strange chiming sound stopped our conversation. Mr. McGregor jumped to his feet as the chimes stopped.

"Is it that late? I am sorry, Kerrie, but I have something I must do."

I felt strange all over the moment the chimes started. Their melody was sweet, but urgent, and I felt I had to be somewhere. I looked up at him confused.

"What were those chimes? I have never heard anything like that before. They were beautiful, and they were calling me to go someplace. I...I don't understand. Where am I supposed to be going?"

He seemed pleased with my confusion. "So you finally heard them did you, child? I suspected long ago that someday you would. It is the summoning of the guardians."

"Those chimes alert us when the first rays of the full moon are upon the meadow. It is time for the accounting. The animals will be waiting for me, so I have no time to explain. I am so sorry, Kerrie, but I must hurry." He said and started toward the door. He picked up an old lamp then stopped and turned around with an odd gleam in his eye.

"Unless you want to come along, child. Perhaps you are suppose to be there."

Before I could comprehend what was happening, I followed him to a nearby meadow. He walked to the center

206

and lit the lantern. I was expecting a bright yellow light but instead a dark blue flame caste a majestic glow over the meadow. I was lost in a daze as I joined him.

"What are we doing here? What did you mean by the accounting?" I whispered.

"Once a year all the forest guardians meet to account for our stewardship. It has been happening for centuries." He whispered back.

Before I could utter another word, an enormous snow owl landed on the ground beside us.

"Alazar, my old friend, I have brought a guest to the accounting this evening. This is Kerrie. She heard the chimes this time." Mr. McGregor greeted him.

"Did she now? Well it is about time you found your apprentice," the owl remarked as he sized me up. He twisted his head one way and then the other.

I gasped and stumbled back when it dawned on me that the owl was speaking. "It is the lantern, Kerrie. Mother Earth left it for us long ago. As long as we stand near the flame the guardians can understand each other," Mr. McGregor explained.

The owl chastised him. "Have you not explained things to her, Alex?"

"There was no time, Alazar. She heard the chimes the same time I did. What was I suppose to do?"

"At least warn her, you old coot," Alazar retorted.

"Hush, you old chicken. I will explain things once everyone is here," Mr. McGregor countered.

Noise echoed in the meadow as animals started to appear from every direction. As the full moon cast its light upon the gathering animals, I felt no fear. I was fascinated to be a witness to something so strange. The hours were lost to me as I listened to animals from the mighty bear to the tiny field mouse give an accounting of their stewardship. Alex McGregor was the last to give his accounting. As he finished speaking, the first rays of the new day touched the meadow.

49

COMING HOME

by
Douglas G. Clarke

I had been gone for too long. Looking from the gate, I could see that no one had picked up the fall's leaves and that now they were covered with winter's first dusting of snow. I paused as I walked up the path when I heard the crunching of the leaves under my feet. Why hadn't Jeffery raked them up?

When I reached the door I saw that there was an envelope tacked to it. The envelope was weathered, and I just stood there looking at it. I finally reached up and gently pulled the nail out, placing it in one of my pockets. I said a few magical words and the nail's hole disappeared as the fibers of the door weaved themselves together.

The note inside read:

Master Gees,

I regret that I could not watch your house as I had told you I would. Something came up, and I had to leave a few weeks after you did. I found someone else to watch your home, and I trust that she did well.

Yours,
Jeffery

I commanded the door to open, and then it closed itself behind me. I looked around the room. In the dim light everything looked just as it had, everything but the source of the dim light.

Sitting on the large oak dinning table was an ornate sliver candlestick, with a tall white candle topped with a yellow flame. The dancing flame was not bright, not bright enough to light the table, but its light somehow lit even the far corners of the room.

I looked longingly at the large leather chair, wanting only to rest, but didn't go to it. Instead I walked around, looking in every room. I wiped my finger along the counter and above the doorsill. Finding no dust, I smiled. Having completed my survey, I returned to the main room.

I was so tired that I decided to figure out what was going on in the morning. I walked to the candle and blew gently on its flame. The flame flickered, but did not go out. I held one hand behind the flame and blew harder. The flame continued to dance. I walked over to the fireplace and retrieved a candlesnuffer. The flame extinguished, As I walked to my bedroom, the flame started dancing again. I sighed and went to bed.

The midnight bell woke me. Normally I would have fallen back to sleep within moments, but a sound from the other room pulled at me and kept me from drifting back to sleep. At first the sound was a clinking. Over time other sounds joined the clinking—the low tone of knocking wood, the high pitch of a finger on the rim of a glass, the noise of a broom. I was half asleep, but as noises grew and formed into a whole, a rising and falling, a melody and harmony, I was drawn awake.

With a start I was fully awake and rose out of bed. The music coming from the other room sounded like it was being created by an orchestra, admittedly a quiet one. I peered into the other room and saw hundreds of flames dancing around the room. Without a thought I called out some magic words and the room was filled with a rushing of wind and all the flame were extinguished, and with them the music.

In the dim light I could see the room was in a shambles. With another sigh, I went back to bed. Twice more the music woke me and, finding my living room engulfed in flames, I put them out. The fourth time I woke, I sat and listened for a while to the music before going into the other room. This time when I looked into the other room I saw the flames, but I had the mind to notice that rather than burning down my house, the flames seemed to be dancing to the music.

I stood there watching the movement of the flames and listening to the beautiful music. I walked to my leather chair, the flames scurrying to get out of my way as I sat down. One final sigh escaped my lips as the flames started dancing on me - straightening my hair, smoothing out the wrinkles in my robe, and pulling the stress from my muscles.

"Jeffery, you trusted well," I said as I drifted back to sleep.

HOUSE GUEST

by
Arlene Lagos

Two months ago I lost the love of my life to a car accident. Jason was struck head-on by a drunk driver, dying instantly. Since then, I haven't been the same. Food is tasteless and dull—when I can manage to keep it down—and sleep has evaded me. My weight has dropped considerably and my head is constantly spinning.

I can't keep lying here day after day, forcing myself to eat, dragging myself out of bed just to try to stay awake so I can stare out the window, hopelessly wondering how I'm going to continue without him. Nothing seems to numb the pain. I feel it all day long, followed by a sleepless night, and then do it all over again. Sometimes I think about just ending it all. Just walking into the ocean as far as I can, putting my head under, opening my mouth, and letting the salt water fill my emptiness.

But, I'd have to sneak past Constantine, the head shrink my mother hired to keep an eye on me. He just showed up one day without notice and moved in! What kind of doctor does that? He's always here, but never says anything. I feel like a prisoner in my own home.

The sun has set now, and I am still staring out the window when a flicker of light coming from Constantine's room catches my attention. With a triple knock, I announce myself, but there's nobody there. Where did he go? I was here all day. Surely I would've seen him leave. There's a blue light glowing from his private bathroom, so I walk in to see what it is. The door shuts behind me, frightening me. Suddenly I hear music playing. It's the sound of children singing lullabies, which I find very creepy. Looking in the mirror, I stare at my reflection. I look tired and sad. My eyes are puffy, and my face is pale. In the background of my reflection I am certain I see Constantine, but my eyes deceive me because when I turn to look, nobody is there.

A chill runs up my spine as I tug on the handle and realize that I can't open the bathroom door. All of a sudden, I hear the shower knobs turning, and the water start pouring into the tub. Picking up the plunger I jam it into the shower curtain, but there is nobody there. Am I going crazy? *Where is Constantine, and why am I locked in this bathroom? Who is doing this?* White with anxiety, I begin to cry, pounding my fists against the wall as the bathroom fills with steam. I slide down the wall onto the floor gasping for air when I look up to see a word forming on the mirror through the steam; M-A-R-C-U-S. Clawing at the walls I start screaming, hoping someone will save me from this nightmare.

"Please don't kill me, I don't want to die!" I scream.

Everything goes dark, and I am certain I am nearing death when I hear a voice.

"Ariana, are you alright?"

When I open my eyes, I am lying in a hospital bed with my mother standing over me.

"What happened?"

"You fainted," she says.

"Oh."

"The doctor ran some tests. He said you were very dehydrated."

"It was Constantine, mom. He was trying to scare me!"

"Who's Constantine?" she says.

"The shrink... the one you hired to live with me?"

"Honey, I never hired anyone to live with you. Are you sure you're alright?"

The doctor comes in with a chart and walks over to me.

"We've put you on a drip to get you hydrated and gave you a little something for the nausea. I've scheduled the OB/GYN to visit this afternoon.

"For what?"

"To make sure everything is okay with the baby."

"I'm... pregnant?"

"Yes. You didn't know?"

A shimmer of light from the hospital window suddenly catches my eye. I turn my head to look out and instead of my own reflection, I see... Jason. He is smiling, surrounded by a glowing blue light. I smile back.

"Adriana, what are you smiling at? Are you okay? Who's this Constantine?"

I look down and place my hands on my stomach, take a deep breath in and exhale. Jason was Constantine and Constantine was Jason. He left me one last thing before he died—a piece of himself, someone to love, a reason to live.

"Marcus," I say proudly.

51

THE OLD HOUSE
THAT I USED TO KNOW

by
Sylvia Stein

Growing up in the town of Brownsville in Texas, I have to say that I was quite happy. I grew up in a 1960s two-story home, that belonged to my grandparents, and which they gladly shared with all of us. I can still recall, I was only seven years old when we moved in with them. I was the oldest of five children. My mother had just packed her bags and left my dad back in San Antonio because she decided that enough was enough!

As my mother planned our new life, my thoughts went back to better days with our dad. I really missed him. He was quite funny, and he had a great singing voice. But sadly, he was a big time alcoholic. Even though he was not violent or ever tried to hurt any of us, he just could not hold a job, and that was the last straw for my mother. I remember walking into the two-story home and being amazed at how clean it was.

"Wow," I told my brother Ramon.

"Grandma sure keeps this house in tip top shape," he called out. He liked to wrestle one of my younger brothers, Ray, to the ground.

"Do you think we will be happy here, Sylvia?" my little sister Francis said.

"I think so," I answered.

But I began to worry about my mother. She was not eating well and, anytime she thought I was not looking, she began to cry. After a couple of months, my mother decided to go see a doctor who could help her through this period in her life. My grandfather did not understand why she had to go and speak to someone else about her problems.

"Come on, Catarina," he said, "you do not want a stranger to know your problems!"

You see my grandfather, Francisco Delgado, immigrated from Mexico to the United States and became a citizen so that he could provide a better life for my mother and her three brothers. He was a loving man, however very much set in his ways.

"Why don't you speak to a priest, mija?" my grandfather added. My grandfather called my mother *mija*, which means *my daughter*.

"Oh, Papa," my mother said, "I have to see a doctor for this!" She stormed out.

After a few months, my mother informed us she was checking into a hospital because the doctors felt she needed to work on herself. Since I was very close to her, I began to cry.

"How long will you be gone? Who is going to take care of us?" I was overwhelmed with pain.

"Oh, baby," my mother said, "please do not cry! I will be back before you know it, and your grandparents are going to take care of you."

My mother left for about six months, which felt like an eternity. In her absence my grandparents did so much for all of us. Feelings stirred inside me when I heard the musical clock in the dining room ring at six o'clock p.m. because it reminded me of a happy sound from another realm. It reminded me of when my mother would make us dinner, and when we sat around the table with my dad before things went bad. Through the years, and all the ups and downs, all of us began to heal.

The happiest moment for me was when my father began rehab and gave up the bottle all together. It was not an easy process, but he was able to kick his habit. As for my mother and his relationship, sadly, they were divorced, but later were able to remain friends.

There were many fond memories in my grandparents' house. They made everything special for all of us. After many years, my grandfather decided to build a new home. It was not an easy one to build. But in the end he wanted us to have something to live in when my grandmother or him passed on.

So in 1995, they began the process of tearing down the old home. I made sure to stop in a few days before the final teardown along with my other siblings, so we could say our goodbyes. I have to say it was emotional and painful. Letting go was not easy. When I think about that old house, I feel an ache in my heart. I light a candle in my home as a reminder of the old house that I used to know.

52

MOHONK LAKE HOUSE

by
Jot Russell

I remember the trip to the lake house as though it was yesterday. And even with a dozen years passed to double my age, I gained no reconciliation from that unbelievable night. As with a needle lodged into my brain, the anniversary of my parents murder brought unavailing memories to the surface of what you might call consciousness. Random waves of thoughts skip across the water. They come and go so freely, but the memory imprisons me back onto the raft that I had used for my escape. The face of the caretaker so etched into my soul. *I know you exist!* How could the police ignore my testimony, and instead take the word of the owner saying there was no such employee?

Fearful from the mystery of dreams to come, I reluctantly succumb to the needs of exhaustion. My bed was just another reminder of loss and loneliness, with my witness of the deed forever repeating within. As my eyes closed, darkness set in like the scene of that eerie hotel. The recollection of my parents' arguments were painted so clear, even when I tried in vain to ignore them. Only the sound of the hotel's music drew me away from their angry words that night so long ago. The echo of instruments within my mind now deepens me into the realm of my imaginary reflection of the past and locks my soul into reliving their death. After a long disturbed sleep, I woke to measure my will to continue this life over the contemplation that builds against me. I wondered if Shakespeare asked himself the question that he so painfully wrote, "To be or not to be?"

Live or die—two choices that I didn't want to answer. Need it be so polar? Do I live in fear of the face I saw or would I die from facing the caretaker? But if I am willing to die, why am I still afraid of just one man? I realized then there was an alternative to my mindless suffering. *I will find you and see what becomes of my fate.*

I suddenly felt awake and alert. Reaching for a morning smoke, I hesitated. This feeling of empowerment was far more pleasing than the method of living in painful memories. I tossed the pack into the trash, but kept my favorite possession in hand. A fancy metallic lighter was all I had left of my parents. The candle's flame flickered, and I took it for the guidance that it continued to provide me. I grabbed what else I needed and headed out.

Off the highway the sight of the watchtower on top of a distant hill ran a chill through my spine. Continuing on, I reached the base and set foot to the long path up the hill. My heart strived to make the climb, pumping the blood that boiled with pain. I rounded the overlook and suddenly paused at the sight—the hotel in its magnificence boasting its presence to the world. I looked toward the entrance, and there he was! Not seeing me at first, the caretaker turned and then caught my gaze. He hesitated, but his eyes squinted in recognition of my now adult face. Suddenly he was gone. I pulled out my knife and quickly gave chase. Seeing a back door swing shut, I followed out and up the walk on the cliff over the lake. "Where are you?" I asked.

"Right behind you!" He growled, and pushed me over the edge.

I plunged into the deep cold water with my knife sinking towards the murky bottom. I gave a gargled curse and struggled my way to shore.

"You can't kill me." He whispered in a voice that seemed to emanate from every direction.

I shot my head around, but he was nowhere to be seen. "Where are you?" I screamed.

"Down here," he whispered.

I slowly gazed down at the water's edge, half realizing what I would find. *My God, he was me all along!* As my head reached the reflection, the caretaker's face displayed instead of my own. From within I cried even as my reflection erupted with maniacal laughter. His face slowly morphed back into my own.

"You're not even real!" I said.

"Then who killed your parents?" he asked.

With a sinking heart, I said, "It was me."

"You couldn't even tie your shoe laces," he said.

A memory triggered in my mind when I was but a child. "I remember you now. I created you to have someone to play with, to teach me things I didn't think I could learn."

"To do things you were afraid to do," he demanded.

"Well, I'm not afraid anymore. And I don't need you."

"Too bad because you can't get rid of me."

"Maybe I can't, but the doctors will help me get rid of you, now that I know what happened, now that I know who you are."

A faint scream echoed in my mind as his consciousness faded. I knew he might return if I did nothing, but the confession of truth to the police and the help of my doctor will eventually drive him away. I looked up towards the watchtower and said, "Mom and Dad, please forgive me."

53

A VOICE IN THE BREEZE

by
Laura Stafford

A stranger answered the door to my house. "Can I help you?" he asked.

I heard a distant fairy tinkling of silver chimes on the night breeze.

* * *

My mother used to put a candle in the window that would flicker and move shadows like some phantom puppeteer. Somewhere far away, silver chimes were singing on the winds that unsettled my curtains.

I remembered her soft china hands stroking my hair and promising me the world, assuring me the monsters of the night would never get into my room. I remembered how fragile her hands looked and how those hands taught me that looks can be deceiving. She had strong capable hands that healed my scraped knees and soothed my hurt soul.

When she died, I saw the doctor put his gentle hands on her forehead, and his hands closed her eyes for the last time. After she died, I longed for her to touch me with her delicate hands and her comforting voice.

Father's hands were much angrier. His hands were roughened by grief and loss, by depression and confusion, by frustration and denial. On the nights that his hands touched me, I couldn't bear to have the candle in the window, silhouetting his looming black figure. The flicker of the candle had lost my mother's warmth.

But on those same nights, I would listen. I would tune my ear to the shimmering music of the silver chimes in the breeze, and I would believe it was my mother singing to me from heaven. And I knew that her song promised me a different future, a better life.

* * *

An eternity later I met Tammy. Her parents were strict and demanding, but not cruel. We didn't have much in common, but she wanted less structure and I wanted more, so we found ourselves together. Her parents were kind to me, allowing me to stay when I needed to get away from my own house. They didn't know my fear, but they could see it. They could empathize with it. And they did something no one else had done since my mother passed. They made me believe I could go to college.

At seventeen years old, I knew I had to find myself, find my own way. Tammy would be going off to college and, although I had a job, it wasn't going to be enough to pay for an apartment, a car, and whatever other bills come along with adulthood.

I applied for better jobs. I searched for the opportunities that would let me make something of myself and help me find my destiny. But there was nothing. I was unskilled. I was qualified to be a janitor and a cashier at a fast food joint.

Why can't I go to college? I wondered. *Am I too afraid to try? Everyone says there are scholarships. Can I get a grant? How do I get financial aid?*

I went to my guidance counselor with my ideas.

"Penn State!" he laughed at me. "That's my alma mater! Don't you think you should try somewhere more... your level?"

* * *

I wanted to hear my mother's silver chimes again, to ease the hurt and pain I felt inside...

Father died last week. I didn't go to the funeral, but he made me the executor of his will. I don't know if it was because I am his daughter, and his only living heir, or if it's because I'm a lawyer now, and he knew I wanted nothing.

The house was sold long ago, just before I started my own practice. I'm not sure why I stood there trying to relieve painful memories. I stared into the bewildered eyes of a stranger in my childhood home. I'm not sure what kind of closure I thought I would find in this place.

Then I heard the silver chimes in the breeze, my mother's voice singing in the darkness.

I could hear my mother's voice speaking to me from heaven.

My mother's beautiful peaceful voice...

"I'm sorry," I tell the stranger in my house. No, it's not my house anymore. It belongs to the stranger. Turning to leave, I said, "I thought I was looking for the past, but I don't need to." *From now on, I'm looking ahead to the future.*

ᗅFTERWORD
by
Jenise Erikson

author of

THE SEA QUEEN

Funny thing about putting pen to paper, or in most cases today, hands to the keyboard, you never know what may become the final product. As creative writers, we craft the product with various ideas to make it as fresh and appealing as possible. I had been playing around with pirate terminology just prior to the prompt for this story due to a few discussions I was having with some friends about Pirate Days—strangely enough, and the story line developed quickly. The Casablanca allusions seemed natural in the context. Time goes by, even for pirates, whence life's more important, affairs overwhelm the simpler needs of cultivating time with that one true love. Sometimes it is not meant to be. Other circumstances take priority no matter how badly we'd rather get lost in a world apart. Aye, that is life - throw in war, and life is indeterminate where love becomes a tragic victim.

ᴀFTERWORD
by
Randy Dutton

author of

SMITHY'S ORGAN

I've been a man of the sea for two tours of duty onboard navy ships. I've even been robbed by a pirate whilst our ship was moored in Subic Bay, Philippines. It wasn't pleasant finding he had climbed aboard our guarded ship and pilfered my wallet while I slept. Pirates tried a second time on a later cruise, but I was prepared. Piracy still happens in the third world, and they're employing new means of luring and attacking travelers. With Smithy's organ, I chose to create a low-tech way to make a siren's call while portraying both a pirate's humanity and viciousness.

ᗅFTERWORD
by
Mike Boggia

author of

THE CARIBBEAN GODDESS

Pirates, treasure, the Bermuda Triangle, and mythological beings are fascinating. Robert Lewis Stevenson's *Treasure Island* drew me in as a child. Rather than gore, this story drew out the mischief in my muse's heart.

AFTERWORD
by
Peter Coster

author of

GET YOUR BOUCANS HERE

Pirates, where do I go with pirates? I thought. I have to admit, partly because I'm in the middle of a pirate novel, currently 120,000 words, and to get things right, I researched. And this research threw up the origin of the terms, buccaneer and filibuster and several others, and somehow this became attached to the concept of celebrity chefs. Don't ask me to explain how. The result is a story that I hope will amuse you while I pass on a little bit of useless information. You never know when seemingly useless information might come in handy.

ᴬFTERWORD
by
Mary Agrusa

author of

A BROTHER'S KEEPER

The pirate theme provided the opportunity to write something other than your typical high seas swashbuckling adventure. I decided to explore the concept that people aren't always who or what we think they are. My pirate became a congenial rogue, willing to help a fellow seaman in distress. Captain Farnsworth's father-in-law, on the other hand, was not the law-abiding, upstanding citizen he portrayed. Farnsworth world is completely turned upside down with the loss of his ship and the discovery that his savior is a half brother to his deceased wife. Add to his grief is the realization that his father-in-law's illegal dealings resulted in the loss of his family. Looks are deceiving at times and can result in disastrous consequences.

ᴀFTERWORD
by Colleen Sayre

author of

SIREN

It's another world in the Abacos where the islands are small and the seafolk rule the waves. They've been guarding their treasure for centuries against the folly of men and the greed of pirates. I've been entranced by the island of Great Guana Cay and it is beautiful beyond belief. But not everything is as it seems when you reach the hidden cays and soft, warm sand—even a pretty girl with long blonde curls washed up on the shore sings a different song of home.

ᗩFTERWORD
by Christian Warren Freed

author of

FROM THE JOURNAL OF
DELBERT THE DREAD

Delbert the Dread is more pun than hero. The lesser, more forgotten son, Dilbert struggles through life in the shadow of his great pirate brother. He's always dreamed to be more than what he is and finds only trouble when he acquires his own ship. While shipwrecked off the coast of Hispanola, Delbert reflects on his brother and the choices he could have done differently. I was inspired by the differences siblings often have and with some of the expression they try to tackle their individual issues. Hopefully you all enjoy as much as I enjoyed exploring it.

AFTERWORD
by
Scott Amis

author of

THE MYSTERIOUS ISLAND

The title for this story is of the book written by Jules Verne, but the concept borrows from *The Most Dangerous Game*, a famous short story written by Richard Connell, first published in 1924. In *The Mysterious Island*, marooned billionaire Davis Wilson comes to face the same odds as did Sanger Rainsford in Connell's story, and takes on his own life-or-death challenge with the same courage and nobility of spirit, but in the end, will he become another version of his captor?

ᴀFTERWORD
by
Arlene Lagos

author of

CALL OF THE SIRENS

As a female writer, I always try to stay away from the typical male-dominated scenario that is constantly flooding our literature, history, and mainstream media. When challenged with the task of writing about pirates, at first I wanted to write about a female pirate. But putting a woman in a natural male role seems out of character. Not that women can't be pirates, but why would we want to be, when we can be so much more? Women are extremely captivating as they are, and so I wanted the story to focus more on what a women would do in a pirate's world. *Call of the Sirens* is about how women have their own useful strengths and survival skills to get what they want and as usual are often underestimated.

AFTERWORD
by
Harry Alexiou

author of

THE HONEYMOONERS

Judging a book by its cover, we've all done it and some would say its human nature. Ricardo's apparent loss is small in comparison to a stranger's who he meets on the otherwise deserted shore and offers him assistance. Tears of sorrow turn to joy as his wife miraculously comes back from the dead. But Ricardo is ultimately guilty of judging a person, by appearance, by small visual snippets which our minds process based on past experience or incorrect assumptions; he is proven wrong by the shoe-less Gerald. The modern day Robin Hood idea is not new but I wanted to link Gerald's loss to real modern day events which touched the hearts of people the world over. His appearance is wrongly judged by the well-to-do honeymooner as one man's selfless crusade endeavours to make the lives of his disaster stricken countrymen more bearable. A saint in a sinners clothing?

AFTERWORD
by
Joyce Shaughnessy

author of

LUCIA

Working with Fiction Writers Guild has been a wonderful experience. It has been a challenge to write a story each month according to the suggested theme, but I've found that I've learned even more from reading stories by other writers. The talented authors on this thread are totally amazing. I feel blessed to have worked with Heather Schuldt because she not only is a great author but is also kind enough to edit and organize these threads for the benefit of us all.

AFTERWORD
by
Gail Harkins

author of

MERGERS & AQUISITIONS

The theme was pirates, but I wasn't prepared to write a swashbuckling tale of the Spanish Main. Modern pirates, then. Perhaps I took leeway, using a successful corporate raider as my pirate? Then again, perhaps not. It was a leap of faith.

This story was inspired by a conversation I overheard several years ago on a sailboat anchored off one of the Tahitian islands. When I amplified the situation into this story, there was a rush of comments. Could the husband really be so callous? Did he utterly lack redeeming qualities? How could a woman just abandon her marriage and walk off with a stranger? Did she ever really love him? For that matter, did he ever really love her? How did she allow her marriage to deteriorate to the point that anything was preferable to the status quo? Was her acceptance given in a fit of pique?

I don't have the answers to all those questions. Relationships are complicated—even fictional ones. However, I like to believe everything will work out for the best.

AFTERWORD
by
Randall Lemon

author of

A MOUSER, A KEG OF RUM, & A GUNNERY MATE

Avast Mateys!! As an avid celebrator on International Talk Like a Pirate Day, how could I resist my chance to get involved in this sea-going volume with a chantey of my own? I drink my grog from a pirate mug and, just prior to writing this Afterword, I finished watching the old film *Captain Kidd*.

A fine crew of writers has gathered together under the Jolly Roger to deliver this fleet of tales for you. Here you'll find treasures to match any that ever sailed the Spanish Main and fell afoul of Blackbeard. Yo-ho-ho!

ᴀFTERWORD
by
H.M. Schuldt

author of

ESCAPING CAPTAIN DRAKE

When introducing a young couple in love, I explored the concept of how explosive it can get when business is mixed with fame and pleasure. I came up with two characters, a talented artist and a smart manager, who find a way to make money in the music industry, but when they are stranded on an island with inmates and pirates, they are faced with a surprising situation: can they work together to find a way off the island before they are found by Captain Drake? A mixture of stubbornness, determination, and competitive natures drive them apart for a short while until admiration and survival bring them back together.

⟨A⟩FTERWORD
by
Lynette White

author of

RECRUITED

The Pirates of old were notorious for being black hearted and ruthless. Is there truth to the legend or are the legends larger than life? Truth is, there are very few written records of a pirate's life but the exploits of pirates such as Blackbeard are well known still today.

I was a young teenager when my history teacher made a profound statement that has always intrigued me. He said "History is dictated by the person telling the story or the man with the pen. Even facts are often at the mercy of the person collecting them."

This story gave me an opportunity to glimpse into the life of a pirate. How did they maintain their crews? How did they get reputations that linger centuries after they are gone? It seems Garth knows.

ᴀFTERWORD
by
Sylvia Stein

author of

THE SCARLETT PRIMUS

The Scarlett Primus is a story about one son's quest to find out what happened to his father and their crew. Captain Shane Hillstrand is missing and so is his crew and now it is up to Leo to try and find out what happened.

In his quest Leo begins to flashback about his father and his closeness with him.

This is a story about the relationship of a son who looked up to his dad and wanted to be just like him, and how he would try and keep his legacy alive.

ᴀFTERWORD
by
Janet Bond

author of

OFF TO THE SEAS

I wrote to the seas to show how people can lose their lives being greedy. Susie and Jack went on a vacation with six other people to relax so they thought. The cruise ship they went on was not like the ship they was suppose to go on. Susie kelp seeing a little boy in the ship for reason, but no one else saw him. The ship had a flag with a skull on it Jack and his friends didn't pay any attraction to it they celebrated it with a drink. Susie started hearing things the boat was pulled in by some force, and she hit her head. She woke up on an island with Jack and the rest of the crew missing.

The same boy she saw on the ship was the same one that would save her. His name was Jimmy he told Susie the boat was hunted before people wanted his treasure, and he tried to won her when she and Jack inter the boat. Jimmy told Susie about the other people on the boat drowned because they was greedy for his treasure and he know it. saved Jack. The deep red sea boat was hunted because people wanted goal.

AFTERWORD
by
Alli Vaughan

author of

JACKIE & THE DEVIL'S DOUBLOON

Pirates are so fun to write about! I loved researching some unique to pirate terms and liked experimenting with their unique speech patterns. I could see this short story expanding into something a little larger, since there aren't many stories of female pirates in the world.

ᴀFTERWORD
by
Mirta Oliva

author of

THIEVES OF THE SEAS

When I was invited to write a Pirates' story for this anthology, I backed off from the laptop. Me and pirates? Inasmuch as these thieves were detestable creatures that left their mark in history books, I had to add some credence to my story, so I did some research. With some facts and permissible distortions as a fiction piece – including not using the word "pirates" – or buccaneers for that matter - I came up with necessary substitutions. In the end, I was delighted to bring my own style to this joint literary effort. Gone be the pirates!

ᴀFTERWORD
by
Elaine Faber

author of

A CAT'S TALE

Pirate stories are often told from the perspective of the captain or the crew. *A Cat's Tale* spins a pirate yarn from the perspective of the ship's working cat, a requirement aboard any ship.

Esme was much sought after for her skill as an expert *ratter*. She would sail only on a ship of her choice, whether legitimate or pirate. Branded as lucky, she became legend for saving a band of kindly but misguided pirates who plundered the seas for pleasure and profit. Esme was a cat seeking the ultimate adventure in a world rife with pirates, rum, gold coins and rats...lots of rats!

PART TWO

ᴀFTERWORD
by
Laura Stafford

author of

LAUGHING FATES

When I think of pirates, I automatically have this vision of rum-swilling, greedy men who rape and pillage, and find pride in that occupation. Jodee, the main character in this story, is an aspiring pirate. When he is faced with the prospects of unlimited wealth, there is no question in his mind what he must do.

Greed is a persistent theme in the world - past and present, fictional and true. The lengths people are willing to go to, the things they are willing to give up for wealth, is always surprising and really rather frightening. Money drives people right out of their minds, a disease that manipulates their capabilities and brings only misery - a lesson Jodee learns all too quickly.

AFTERWORD

by
Neil Carroll Ellison

author of

SALVATION

I don't like predictable stories. Why would I (or my readers) want to invest time in a tale to which I (or they) can, with little effort, guess the outcome? Challenge me. Throw me off track. Make me think. Surprise me. I considered titling this story *Here There Be Monsters* but felt that it would telegraph the ending. Instead, I wanted to focus on the nature of salvation both big and small. Is salvation the opportune sighting of an island while lost at sea or is it meeting a fellow castaway? Could it be found in denouncing humanity and living by one's own devilish code? Is it an ultimate outcome for which we pray? Is it all or none of these things? Could one seeming salvation lead us out of a proverbial frying pan and into a real fire?

ᴀFTERWORD

by
Glenda Reynolds

author of

WITCH'S ISLAND

Portions of the *Witch's Island* short story came from *The Cursed Leviathan* volume 2 of the Goddess of the Moon Saga, which is currently being written. The *Twilight* character Laurent and the notoriety of Black Beard inspired me to do a Jamaican vampire named Captain Jon Devon, the devil. I wanted to elaborate on the setting in which the main characters came under their curse. I also received inspiration from a picture on the internet of a smooth-barked tree on a beach and from a second picture of a lighthouse amidst black craggy boulders.

AFTERWORD
by
Timothy Paul

author of

THE TENTH GOLD PIECE

From the swashbucklers of early films to Disney's Captain Jack Sparrow, pirate tales have been characterized by enchantment, colorful costumes, and flamboyant rascals. Magical elements are woven throughout this story from the mystical tune that carries a villain back in time to his transformation into a historical figure. With nods to a few icons from my youth, an anti-hero makes the choice that saves his life and dooms him to serve penance on the high seas.

ᴀFTERWORD
by
Douglas G. Clarke

author of

FINDERS KEEPERS

When I started to think about writing a pirate story, I tried to figure out what relationship the man and woman should have. I don't want to write about a typical womanizing man, so I turned the story around and wrote about a manizing woman. With that twist in mind, I wrote the story with the effort to keep this twist hidden till the end. I like how it ended up. A man kept himself alive for three years, not trusting anyone, only to be lead to ruin by a beautiful woman.

ᴀFTERWORD

by
Clement Chow

author of

THE TECHNICIAN

When writing this short story, consideration was given to the concept of piracy and to the reader's mindset. The aim was to appeal to the widest possible audience; the ongoing conflict with Somali pirates was therefore chosen. The intent was to show the personal side of the "ocean robbers" and the Combined Task Force that fights them. Each robber or soldier has his/her own reason to join the trade. Family was chosen as the motivating factor in this story, but there can be a multitude of other factors as well. At the end of the day, both robbers and soldiers have their own stories.

ᗩFTERWORD

by
Connie Flanagan

author of

MAROONED!

When asked to write a story about pirates without using the word *pirate*, I was a little daunted. At first I was tempted to use modern day pirates; I realised, however, that using stereotypes of old-fashioned pirates would render it easier to indicate the profession of these dastardly individuals. Not wanting my story to be a mere copy of Disney, however, I decided to play with the possible double meaning of *ship* by having a star ship and an extraterrestrial explain the alleged curse of music that draws in sea faring ships. I hope that readers of *Marooned* enjoy this twist.

ᴀFTERWORD

by
Oliver Dolan

author of

DIGGITY ISLE

Diggity Isle is a story about one of those dreams that seems so real, is so vivid, and at the same is utterly disturbing. We've all had them - the ones where you wake up and wonder how your mind could possibly concoct such a grim tale. In this case, Murray dreams of a plane crash where he and his sister are the lone survivors, and he's responsible for getting them back to civilization safely. Trust is another central theme here, highlighting the fact you have to be careful with whom you place your trust, especially in the case of pirates!

ᴀFTERWORD
by
Shelly Heskett Harris

author of

BUCCANEER DAYS

The protected kleptomaniac football-player is true. I loved the premise of a town-wide conspiracy for a high school activity. It was so Texan I knew I had to use it sometime. This seemed perfect.

Since Buccaneer Days is authentic, I needed to make sure the fictional school and hotel were obviously made-up. Hence the name, Obama High School.

Cabbagehead is a kind of jellyfish. If it bumps into you, it leaves painful spikes in your skin. The fish have been known to clog up the shoreline enough to stop swimming.

You might see these bounty hunters again.

AFTERWORD

by
Rebecca Lacy

author of

A SHIP OUT OF TIME

I wrote this shortly after watching a program debunking the theory that the Bermuda Triangle is some mysterious trap for unwary airplanes and ships. The fact it may not be UFO's luring these hapless vessels to their doom doesn't make the area any less ripe for fictional adventure, in my mind. Thus, I thought it might be fun to see what would happen if two ships from different centuries enter the triangle at the same time. I enjoyed meeting my two characters and think there is a possibility that they could get into all kinds of mischief in a novel. What do you think?

Afterword

by
Robert A. Strobel

author of

ADRIFT

When I was asked to write a pirate story I was thrilled to no end, I searched about my mind I remembered that mutineers were infamous for setting their captains adrift upon the open sea. Dating a British girl long ago helped out immensely. Remembering the conversations we had was a hoot. So I capitalized on this fact and set forth to write of the events that led up to the captains quandary. I tried to inject some humor into a hopeless situation by imagining what would I do in the captain's place, Understanding where he came from.

AFTERWORD

by
JD Mitchell

author of

MIGRATING ISN'T STEALING

During the last few years, I have written various storylines that have been sitting around in my head ever since I first started playing around with cut-n-paste collages. Writing short stories has been anything else but natural, however. *Migration Isn't Stealing* is luckily a stand-alone story from a story arc I've long envisioned.

ᴀFTERWORD
by
A.L. Scott

author of

REMINISCING

I enjoy imagining scenarios that lead down one path, only to close at an unexpected end. Weaving twists and turns into the fabric of storytelling is something I'm always keen to expand. There were many pirate stories in my head, but I finally decided to go in the opposite direction.

Robert would come across as a semi washed-up pirate of old, right from the start by virtue of his walks down memory lane and accoutrements d'œuvre (tools of the trade). But really, he's more of a *wannabe*.

This story hopes to tap into our occasional need to make believe we're someone or something we're not.

AFTERWORD
by
D.B. Martin

author of

THE WRECK OF THE CONARY

The Wreck of the Conary was formed by the format laid down by Writers 750 along with two loves of mine—the tales of Blackbeard and my love for surprise endings. I generally write for children, but I do have a novel coming out in 2014. I hope all who read *The Wreck of the Conary* and other stories from this anthology find enjoyment and intrigue.

ᴀFTERWORD
by
DC Mills

author of

ABANDONING SHIP

Sometimes, losing your way means finding a new and wholly unexpected path.

James and Jakob had their careers in commercial transport secured, until their ship crashed; now, they are heading for new adventures aboard a fast ship under an enigmatic captain. The two of them seem not quite agreed on how to approach this new opportunity. And how will the company regard the disappearance of a barge and its valuable cargo?

ᴀFTERWORD
by
Amos Parker

author of

CAPTAIN

I worked for a long time with a lot of writers from my writing group to get this story full of the most interesting stuff I could. I had a great time making things big and wild, dramatic and overblown. Heather's suggestion to make things into *Giant Tales* was a big part of that. The pirates are sort of giant, as you can tell. And turning evil can make people have giant impacts and giant egos. Plus, pirates are just plain awesome.

ᴀFTERWORD
by
JZ Murdock

author of

BREAKING ON CAVE ISLAND

Breaking on Cave Island has a curious evolution. Having never written a pirate story, I troubled over it all day till bedtime, then woke the next morning watching it play out in my head like a movie; I had merely to write it down. A few drafts later that day, I sent it off.

Lord Ritchie's character has been around since the early 1980s from the original story, *Poor Lord Ritchie's Answer to a Question He Knever Knew*, eventually published in my book, *Anthology of Evil* (2012). Before that in 2004, actor Rutger Hauer chose that story as a winner in an international short story contest.

This new story is therefore a prequel to Ritchie's later, less sanguine adventures and also gives insight to his attitude toward wizards. I had a lot of fun writing this tale, especially knowing that Ritchie is now more than he has ever been before, and his legacy continues to grow.

AFTERWORD
by
Jot Russell

author of

MOHONK LAKE HOUSE

The unbounded nature of the human psyche can lead us to believe any of the dark lies that we tell ourselves in cooping with the painful truths of life. As a child, my character's pain was caused by the continual bickering of his parents. A pain that built until that unbelievable night when he could bare it no more. With the misfire of synapse, a new schizophrenic consciousness was spawned and provided him a means to erase the pain. Little did he know that this alter ego would alter his memory and instill hatred toward an evil that lay quietly within him. As an adult, the realization that their blood was on his hands cast a light toward a narrow path of needing to face the truth.

ᗩFTERWORD
by
Steve Bridger

author of

X-treme

The challenge in writing *X-treme* was to weave an intensely suffocating choice of words and phrases to first attract and absorb the reader into the experience. The aim was for the reader to have all five senses stimulated by the situation, the darkness, the lack of air, the stinging sharpness of pine, skin shivering with cold, scratched and helpless, as if they were living the horror themselves, to cause a physical reaction direct from the page to the brain.

PROFESSOR LIMN BOOKS

GIANT TALES:
Beyond the Mystic Doors
From the Misty Swamp
World of Pirates

CRYSTAL SWORD CHRONICLES:
GRYFFON MASTER

For more information
please visit

writers750.com